Christmastime 1946

A Love Story

LINDA MAHKOVEC

Other books by Linda Mahkovec

The Garden House

And So We Dream

The Notebooks of Honora Gorman:
Fairytales, Whimsy, and Wonder

The Christmastime Series

Christmastime 1939: Prequel to the
Christmastime Series

Christmastime 1940: A Love Story

Christmastime 1941: A Love Story

Christmastime 1942: A Love Story

Christmastime 1943: A Love Story

Christmastime 1944: A Love Story

Christmastime 1945: A Love Story

Valentine's Day 1946: Sequel to the
Christmastime Series

Short Collections

The Dreams of Youth

Seven Tales of Love

Design and distribution by Bublish

ISBN: 979-8-89989-064-2 (paperback)
ISBN: 979-8-89989-065-9 (eBook)

Historical note:

When World War II began, the U.S. faced a massive labor shortage as millions of men went off to fight. Women were asked to step into jobs that had once been off-limits to them. Around six million more women joined the workforce, bringing the total to nearly 19 million – about one in three women working outside the home.

Before the war, women were mostly limited to service roles – teaching, nursing, clerical work, or domestic jobs. But by 1945, they were building tanks and airplanes, welding in shipyards, operating heavy machinery, managing offices, and keeping the country running at home while the fighting continued overseas.

When the war ended, they were expected – or pressured – to give up these jobs and return to their old roles. Still, their contributions were critical to the war effort and helped pave the way for future advances for women.

Chapter 1

Lillian looked at the spread of drawings for her upcoming meeting at Haden with Mrs. Huntington. Women in the workforce. She pulled out the three strongest – a medical researcher in a lab, an architect's assistant at a drafting table, and a newspaper reporter conducting an interview – and felt a thrill of accomplishment.

If it all came through, this assignment would be the high point of her career as an artist, the culmination of long years of honing her craft. The theme was perfect for her, and she felt up to the task.

She was grateful that Mrs. Huntington had encouraged her to visit several offices and job sites over the past two years. The non-traditional jobs that women had filled during the war had, for the most part, been reclaimed by returning soldiers.

But these working women images and the novels about them would make solid book covers and would be sure to sell. Mrs. Huntington understood that women would be interested in reading about such characters – capable women full of determination, who took pride in their work.

Lillian had just put Charlotte down for a nap and looked over at Charles and the boys. She smiled to see Gabriel and Tommy sitting next to him, rapt with attention as he recounted information about the Roman empire. One of the best things about the war being over was that Charles was able to spend time with the boys. Weekends, nights, a few family trips. And after school times like now, helping Tommy with his assignment.

She tilted her head and realized how similar Charles and Tommy were – serious, quiet, with a love of learning. She was somewhat surprised that Tommy was so taken with the subject – or maybe it was Charles's way of explaining it.

She took her coat from the closet and slipped it on, and used the hall mirror to position her hat.

Charles raised his head. "Going outside?"

"I need to walk off some of my energy – I'm bursting with ideas!"

He was mildly surprised. "I thought you'd be tired. You stayed up late, got up early…"

Lillian laughed at herself. "It's been a while since I've felt so fired up over an assignment. A *possible* assignment," she corrected herself.

"I think this calls for a celebration."

"If all goes well, I couldn't agree more." She leaned down and kissed his cheek. "I'll find out more at the next meeting. But Mrs. Huntington is behind the idea and she wants me – my illustrations." Lillian tucked her grocery list into her purse. "Monday will be the first time the new director, Mr. Borland, will be heading the meeting. I'm a little nervous."

Tommy set his pencil down and looked up. "Isn't Mrs. Huntington the head?"

"She's been the force behind the book department for the past ten years, though it has changed so much recently. Still, I'd say it's a go. Women in the workforce. A whole series. She has several authors lined up, women she has worked with for years. It reminds me of the campaign I worked on at Rockwell Publishing. I have the same kind of enthusiasm."

"You liked the boys' adventure book, too," said Gabriel. "That was fun."

"I loved it. The past two years have been mostly children's books, but I do welcome this change. The war taught me so much about the untapped abilities of women." She thought of the past few years and the changes they had brought. "Women did everything. From the day-to-day work of bus drivers, barbers, and mail deliverers. To the skilled jobs of machinists and engineers, pilots, and codebreakers. I feel honored to be able to represent some of that spirit."

"And don't forget the spies!" added Gabriel.

"Ohhh, that would make a good book cover." She ruffled his hair and pulled her gloves on. "I'll just make a quick trip to the store, while Charlotte is sleeping."

"I'll come," said Gabriel, jumping to his feet.

She didn't know whether Charles had given a subtle sign for the boys to help her, or whether Gabriel's interest in Roman military campaigns had reached saturation point. He had been enthralled hearing about elephants crossing the wintry Alps, but the ensuing battles and rebellions lacked the high drama he so loved.

"I can help," Tommy offered. But Lillian could see that he didn't want to leave in the middle of Hannibal's stunning invasion.

"No, no. Stay and do your homework. I only have a few things to get for dinner. I really just feel like getting some air."

Tommy settled back into the story, and Lillian and Gabriel slipped out the door.

Gabriel pressed the elevator button and when the doors opened, cried, "I'll race you!"

He always preferred taking the stairs, as did Lillian, but today she indulged him in the race and stepped into the elevator.

When the elevator doors opened in the lobby, there stood Gabriel, calmly leaning against the wall with his arms folded, as if he had been waiting for quite some time.

"You win again," said Lillian. "And there was only one stop for the elevator. You must have flown!"

Gabriel grinned at the comment and rushed to opened the front door.

Lillian noticed the signs of Christmas in the brownstones across the street, where the fading afternoon revealed a few strings of lights in the windows. "Look, Gabriel. People are already decorating for Christmas."

"We have to get our tree soon." He looked from the decorations in the windows to a few doors with wreaths.

"Yes, we will," Lillian said, wondering when she could find the time. "The nights have been so busy, lately. Between your Scouts activities, and our volunteering at the hospital –"

"Oh!" Gabriel snapped to attention, startling Lillian. "I forgot to tell you! Guess who I saw in the park?"

Lillian gave a shake of her head.

"Happy. Hap. You know, from the hospital. Remember him?"

It took Lillian a moment, then it clicked. "Oh, Hap. Harrison Coleman. Of course I remember him. He was discharged last year. What was he doing in the park?"

"Just sitting, not far from the hot chocolate vendor I go to, you know, by the pond. Hap told me he goes there because it's quiet. He checks for jobs in the morning at the VA boards. If he can't find work, he goes to the park. He says it's better than sitting in his boarding house. And he doesn't like all the stores and shoppers."

"Hmm. Coleman." Lillian's brow pinched in perplexity. "His name came up recently. The last time I was there." She searched her memory but came up empty. "Someone was looking for him, I think. Or making inquiries. I can't remember."

Gabriel was already on to the next idea. "Can we go the long way?"

Lillian had to smile. That meant passing by their old apartment. As much as they loved their new home, it was always a pleasure to walk down the block where they had lived for several years and to perhaps bump into any of their old neighbors.

"Of course."

At the next block they turned onto their old street. Lillian saw Mrs. Wilson up ahead, walking in her usual brisk manner. She was too far to call out to her, and Gabriel was in the middle of a story involving Mr. G and the Red String Curio Store, so Lillian simply observed her as she listened to Gabriel. There was something distinctly different about Mrs. Wilson, though Lillian couldn't put her finger on what it was. A restlessness? An air of distraction?

Lillian watched as her old neighbor stopped at the corner, looked one way, then the other – and then gazed down at the ground, as if lost in thought. She continued walking, then abruptly turned around and came back towards them.

"Huh," said Lillian, puzzled by her manner.

"What Mom? Are you listening? Mr. G said we have to start decorating for Christmas."

Lillian draped her arm around Gabriel. "Yes, Christmas will be here before we know it. I was just watching Mrs. Wilson. She must have forgotten something."

Their old neighbor was almost upon them, but was still so deep in thought that she didn't notice them until Lillian greeted her.

"Oh, hello there, Lillian, Gabriel!" The worry on her face vanished as she smiled. "I didn't see you. I was just… Where are you off to?"

"Just getting a few things for dinner."

Mrs. Wilson leaned towards Gabriel. "And how are you? How's school? How's your job?"

"My job is swell," answered Gabriel, relieved that she didn't pinch his cheek like she used to. "I'm getting out all the red and green things, and anything to do with Christmas – reindeer, bells, angels and stars, creche sets – we have five this year – and Santa Claus, of course."

Mrs. Wilson smiled indulgently at Gabriel. "It's that time of year. The onslaught of Christmas shoppers will soon be upon us all. I'll stop by the Red String soon. See if I can find anything for Harry."

"And where are you going, Mrs. Wilson?" Lillian asked.

"Oh, just – nowhere, really, just thought I'd…" She glanced around. "Well, time to get started on dinner, I suppose." She tightened her headscarf and gestured back down the street a bit. "Good thing you're walking this way. I just saw Billy sitting outside on the stoop. Looks like he could use some cheering up." She waved goodbye and hurried on.

Lillian sensed the unease under Mrs. Wilson's words and wondered at the source. Then she noticed that Gabriel was watching Mrs. Wilson with a studied expression.

"What? What are you thinking, Gabriel?"

Gabriel nodded at the conclusion he had come to. "She's not happy like she used to be."

"Mrs. Wilson? What do you mean?"

Gabriel gave a shrug. "She was happier during the war." He saw that Lillian was about to object and clarified his thought. "I don't mean she liked the war. But I think she liked what she did. I think she misses her job with the city."

Lillian glanced back. Mrs. Wilson had already gone inside her brownstone. "Hmm. You may be right, Gabriel. Mrs. Wilson has so much energy and loves to be busy. I think her position at the Board of Transportation suited her. But I also think she's relieved to be home more. Everyone is."

"Yep! That's for sure. Dad's home every day now."

"No more waiting and guessing and worrying. I'm so glad those days are over." Lillian gave a deep sigh at the recent memories.

Gabriel looked up ahead and spotted his best friend. "Hiya, Billy!"

There was Billy, sitting on the top step of the brownstone building, with his chin cupped in his hands. Looking rather dejected, just as Mrs. Wilson had described him.

"Hi, Mrs. Drooms. Heya, Gabe."

"Hello, Billy," said Lillian. "Aren't you cold sitting outside?"

"Nah. I got some thinking to do. It's quieter out here."

Gabriel turned to Lillian and spoke just above a whisper. "I think he needs me, Mom. Can I sit with him while you shop?"

"Of course. I'll just be a few minutes." She turned to Billy. "You're welcome to come back with us, if it's fine with your mother."

Billy gave a limp shrug. "Nah. I got some chores to do. Thanks, anyway, Mrs. Drooms."

Gabriel ran up the steps. "I'll wait for you here, Mom." He sat next to his old pal and nudged him. "What's up, Billy? You look down in the dumps."

Billy breathed out a long pent-up sigh, and turned his mouth down on one side. "Money problems."

"Oh no!" Gabriel sat up, worried. "Your parents?"

Billy jerked his head back. "No. Me!"

"Oh." After a moment, Gabriel added, "What do you need money for?"

"You know what. Classes. I mean *real* classes, not just squeezed-in makeshift lessons." Billy's success in school plays over the years had whetted his appetite for acting. Over the past year it had turned into a passion. "Mom and Dad say spending money on acting classes is a waste. But how else can I learn?"

"What does Mickey say? Is he on your side?"

Billy blew out a puff of air and gave a good imitation of his older brother. "Of all the jobs out there, you pick acting? What are you, nuts?"

Gabriel sighed. Sometimes Tommy was on his side. Sometimes not. "I have ten dollars I saved from my job. Would that help?"

Billy gave a hint of a smile. "Thanks, Gabe. What I need is a job. A way to make some money." He glanced over at Gabriel. "A real job."

Gabriel nodded in understanding. For the past few months, whenever he could find some free time, Billy had been helping out at a small cabaret a few blocks over. Sweeping floors, cleaning windows, and polishing glasses for the evening's show, in exchange for a few lessons – acting, singing, tap dancing, whatever was available – he wasn't picky. He wanted to learn everything he could about the business. But when his parents discovered how he was spending his time, they put a stop to it.

Billy shook his head and gave a dramatic sigh. "I loved that job. I was getting good. Well, kind of good. At tap dancing, anyway. It made me want to learn even more."

"I know the feeling. I almost had to give up my job at the Red String. Woulda killed me. Maybe you could convince your parents?"

Billy gave a snort. "I've given up. I tried every argument I could think of. They said the cabaret is an *unwholesome* environment for kids. But I'm not a kid. I'm thirteen now. That makes me a teenager."

They sat quietly for a while, Billy, looking morose, Gabriel's mind running through possible solutions. He threw his hands out and gave Billy a light smack.

"Billy, this is New York! There must be hundreds of jobs out there. Maybe thousands! Even with all the soldiers back and looking for work. Sure, most jobs are for adults, but there are plenty of jobs for kids. Especially teenagers like you. Just keep looking."

"Yeah, I'll think of something. I'm not giving up, that's for sure."

Gabriel decided that to lift Billy's spirits, he would talk about acting. "Just remember, you're the boss of you. Class or no class, you can still work on your acting. What about a skit for the school Christmas show? We still have time to hand in an idea."

"Yeah, maybe."

Gabriel was surprised at Billy's lukewarm response. "We've done it every year! We can't miss this year. How about it? It'll be fun."

Billy shrugged, uninspired. "I don't know."

"You could add it to your list of acting experience."

"My list of parts!" A spark of interest finally came to Billy's eyes. He gave it some thought, nodding slowly. "You're right. I need more experience to help fill up a page. Even a short school skit counts. Got any ideas?"

"Let me think about it. I'll come up with some ideas and you can pick which one you want. Deal?"

"Deal." They shook hands and started talking about how much time they had to come up with a subject and how much rehearsal time they would need. They decided to keep it to just the two of them, to simplify it.

"You'll be the star, Billy. I'll be the director or manager or whatever."

By the time Lillian returned with her groceries, the two boys were standing and laughing, trying out some of their impersonations they used to torment Tommy and Mickey with.

Billy stood at the top of the steps while Gabriel ran down to take the bag of groceries from Lillian.

"Tomorrow, Gabe! Bye, Mrs. Drooms."

"Sure thing!" Gabriel said.

In response to Lillian's raised eyebrows, Gabriel began filling her in on the school's Christmas show.

"Hey, Gabriel!" Billy called out after them. "The theme for this year's program is patriotism."

"Piece of cake!" hollered Gabriel, his mind sparking with possible ideas.

Chapter 2

Izzy glared at the silent phone on the counter, then shifted her eyes up to the clock. 2:25. She was beginning to hate Saturdays.

True, it had been her idea to work at Red's family business on Saturdays, to get a feel for the job, ease herself into a possible role in the construction business. She worried about Red and his quiet moods. She thought that working together would be a way to keep an eye on him. But she now realized that their paths wouldn't cross as she had imagined. He was often out in the field, at construction sites, and inspecting possible locations with his two older brothers, his uncle, and cousins. Only sometimes helping out his father with accounting issues at the office. At the other end of the building.

Besides, this office work did not suit her. It was nothing like her vibrant role at Rockwell Publishing. She had assumed it would include some degree of stimulation and challenge, but as far as she could tell, it was limited to answering the phone and taking messages. Her two sisters-in-law were more than capable and didn't seem to feel the bone-grinding boredom that plagued her Saturdays.

The eldest one, Dotty, sat filing her nails as she described the latest shopping spree she took with the other sister-in-law.

"So, I says to Babs, I says, 'Sorry to say it, kid, but that color does not like you. And she says, still admiring herself in the mirror, 'It's called tangerine dream.' I says, 'Nightmare, more like. It adds a good ten pounds and with that busy pattern, well, you look like an overstuffed armchair.' And she says, 'Are you hinting I need to lose weight?' Ha! Me, hint? It was a losing battle. At that point I says, 'Let's go get some coffee and cake…' Dotty lifted her eyes from her nails. "Are you listening, Izzy? Izzy!"

"Yes, cake. If that damned phone doesn't ring in the next five minutes, I'm chucking it out the window!"

"Oh, you're such a card!" Dotty laughed and laughed. "That's what I love about you, Iz, you're just so funny! Babs is jealous that I get to spend most Saturdays with you. I told her, just you wait. Izzy will soon be working full time, if *I* have anything to say about it. Though I do hope you keep Saturdays. Keep me company. One or two days a week is all I want. But we need another person in the office. I've been here for five years and let me tell you it has never been busier."

"Then why does it feel so dead?"

"Because it's Saturday! You card. Or is it cad? Let me tell you, when I used to work during the week, I could hardly keep up. I'd come in the office, run around like a chicken with its head cut off." She scrunched up her face. "I never really liked that image. Anyway – answering the phones, scheduling meetings, processing invoices, oh my! I'd be breathless!" She pressed her hand on her chest. "The next thing I knew it was time to go home! Now with the men back in the office…"

"Do you miss it?"

"Miss it! Not on your life. Not for a minute! I can be a proper wife now. Take the car shopping, see what other women are wearing, get my hair done regularly." She patted her latest hairstyle. "Then I love cooking, trying out the latest recipes, oh, and we're going to renovate our kitchen, and then, let me tell you, I'll be baking up a storm. My sis stopped by yesterday. Or was it the day before, I can't remember. Anyway, she was telling me about a new recipe and yakyakyak laughlaughlaugh snortchucklegasp…She thinks he might be cheating on his wife because he's always all spruced up."

Izzy's head snapped up. "Who?"

"Her neighbor! Two doors down, across the street. Aren't you listening?"

Izzy saw that it was only 2:45. "How is that possible," she groaned.

"Oh, it's possible all right. And it wouldn't be the first time, according to her."

Izzy jumped to her feet, looked around for something, anything, to do. She took her glass of water and poured it on the potted plant in the window.

"You're going to kill it! That's two glasses you dumped on it after I already watered it this morning." Dotty put the nail file into the pencil cup, and fanned out her fingers, turning her head from one side to the other to assess the color. "This is the shade you recommended. What do you think?"

Izzy stared at the shiny red nails. "Very nice. The color matches the polka dots on your dress."

"It does, doesn't it! Red makes a nice change from the coral, don't you think? I like coral for summer. And pink. Pink is nice for summer and spring."

Izzy shot to her feet. "I need to do something, Dotty."

Dotty blinked her eyes in surprise, and then waved her away. "Well, go right ahead, Izzy. I'll cover for you. You know that."

"No, I mean – I need to work. To keep busy. I don't feel like I'm doing anything."

Dotty let out a laugh. "You just paid three invoices and finished up on all the filing! That would have taken me a week. Sit down and relax."

Izzy dropped back into her chair.

"So, I need your opinion, Izzy. Your honest opinion. Babs and I are planning the company Christmas party – you'll be there – and we're trying out new recipes for snacks to pass around when people first arrive. I say we go with mini meatballs and cocktail sausages, but Babs insists on anchovy paste on rye and deviled eggs…"

Izzy stifled a yawn and wished Red would stop by. Or call. As she listened to the descriptions of olives and pickled vegetables and crackers and toast spreads and stuffed celery, she reorganized her desk. Restacked the papers. Sharpened the pencils. Organized the tray with paper clips, staples, and rubber bands. *Don't do it*, she told herself. *Don't do it.* But her eyes went to the clock again. 3:08.

What had she been thinking? Why had she envisioned lunches with Red, leaving for home together, strategizing with him on the business! Was she crazy? They didn't need her for that. They didn't even seem to need Red for that. They had been running the business for years without either one of them.

She had been hoping to love it here as much as at Rockwell Publishing. But she didn't. Maybe she was being unfair. It was Saturday, after all. Again and again, she had tried to envision herself working full time here – but she just couldn't make the leap to actually do it. She knew that once she left her job at Rockwell Publishing, she would never get it back again. The market was now flooded with eager workers.

No easy answers. Nothing sounded right. As she listened to Dotty, she started to dust the top of the filing cabinet. "Yes, yes, I'd go with the salmon mousse – sounds delicious."

An accidental look at her watch. 3:27.

Dotty stood up and stretched. "I love Saturdays. Gives me a chance to relax – and chat with you! Can you watch the phone? I'm going to fix myself a cup of coffee. Want some?"

"Got any whiskey you can add to it?" asked Izzy.

"Oh, you cad! Or is it card? You're a real stitch!" Dotty's laughter trailed after her down the hall. "Whiskey!"

Izzy stood before the window and stared out at the street traffic below. "I can't do this," she said softly.

The rest of the afternoon was spent listening to Dotty read from the magazine she flipped through. "Oh, doesn't she look smart in that outfit? That suit would look good on you, Iz. And these lip colors! Gorgeous. Course, anything would look good on Judy Garland. Don't you just love her?"

Dotty turned a few more pages, commenting on the articles. "*Should You Tell Them There's a Santa Claus?* Absolutely! *Man is a Miracle.* I'll say. *Cash Contest for Cooks.* Ooh, maybe I should enter my coconut chiffon cake. I add red and green candied cherries to make it look Christmassy."

"You should, Dotty. No one can bake a cake like you."

"Aren't you a doll. Maybe I will." She turned another page and leaned in closer to read. "*Give Her Something for Her Christmas Table.* Or closet. Oh, here we go! *How to throw a party.* Listen to this…"

Then, finally, "4:50, already! Where did the time go?" Dotty closed the magazine and reached for her handbag. "Time to powder my nose, don't want to be late. We're going out for a bite. I know you'll dart out of here right on the dot, so I'll say goodbye now." She put her cheek next to Izzy's, and hurried down the hall. "Say hello to Red!" she called behind her, wiggling her fingers in the air.

Just as Izzy was slipping on her coat, Red entered the office. She ran into his arms as if she had been rescued. "Red!"

He gave a laugh and embraced her. "Hey, hey! What's all this?"

"Get me out of here, Red. Please! Let's go out to dinner."

"I was just thinking the same thing."

Izzy grabbed her purse and hat, and they were soon hailing a cab on the avenue.

They went down to the Village to one of their favorite restaurants. Over eggplant parmigiana, chicken cacciatore, and a bottle of chianti, she finally relaxed and tried to express her mixed feelings.

"Everything feels so different, Red. I'm not sure I'm right for the family business."

"Sure, you are. Dotty loves you. They all do."

"I love them too. Dotty makes me laugh, and Babs is real sweet. But... I don't feel – needed. I don't really do anything."

Red took her hand. "So, give it up. You love Rockwell Publishing. You always have. Stay there."

He held up his other hand as she began to protest. "I know we thought working together would be a good thing for us. But chances are our paths wouldn't cross anyway. You might as well be where you want to be. Where you love the work itself." Red gave her a big smile.

Izzy nodded slowly but was unconvinced. Then she leaned forward and took a closer look at Red. "Is it my imagination, or are you happy about something?"

He laughed and took a sip of wine. "Yes. I do have good news. Great news, in fact."

Izzy's eyes lit up in hope. "What? What is it?"

"You remember me talking about Sanchez?"

"Sanchez… The ball turret gunner, right? From Texas." Izzy hadn't seen Red so animated and happy for a long time and smiled in anticipation.

"He's in town. I got a message from him today, asking to meet him for lunch." Red's face filled with a special warmth that always came when he talked about the men from his crew. "It was so good to see him. To catch up. Anyway, one thing led to another and turns out he's looking for work. Is considering settling in New York."

"And?" Izzy asked, hopeful.

"I told him maybe I could find him something with our company. He's a smart guy – focused, dependable – can count on him for anything."

"Do you think they'll…" She left her question unasked, and gave a smile. "That would be wonderful, Red."

"We're expanding every day and could really use a guy like him."

"That is good news, indeed." She raised her glass and took a sip. "To our friends."

"And to each other," he said, and leaned across the table to give her a kiss.

Chapter 3

Mason chuckled to himself as he made his way home after work. He was happy to see Mrs. Sullivan back in the office after her "retirement" that had lasted all of six months. She had been working all her life, and he had wondered how she would take to not coming into the office anymore. She was a worker through and through – not to mention an integral part of Drooms Accounting for more than twenty-five years. Drooms & *Mason* Accounting, formally, he thought with fondness. Charles Drooms and Mrs. Sullivan had formed the cornerstone of his career.

When she left six months ago, there began a slow decline in the running of the office. Nothing major. Misplaced files, delays in follow up with outside matters, running out of supplies. Little things, for the most part.

But more recently, the mood of the place had changed. There was no reason for it. Their business, as well as the general economy, was surging. Happiness was in the air! The war was over, most of the men were now home, rationing – except for sugar – was at an end, and everything was now available. In abundance! Life was easier. And Christmas was just weeks away.

Yet, there was a sense of unease in the office. He felt it. Less laughter, less joking around, fewer smiles. Clashes in personalities. Things they never had to worry about in the past. They hadn't realized just how much Mrs. Sullivan was responsible for keeping things running smoothly.

Mason couldn't be sure, but he had a feeling that a few of the newly hired men – two in particular – were part of the problem. Eric Clay had been rehired on his return. He had left in 1942 when he was drafted. Mason had never cared for him. He was a troublemaker back then. The war had only seemed to make him worse – dictatorial, judgmental. A bully. Then to add to the problem, Eric had convinced Charles to hire his army buddy, Bo Creeley. Said it was the patriotic thing to do.

Mason thrust his hands in his pockets. Maybe his simple dislike for them was clouding his judgment. He couldn't be sure if he was clearly assessing the situation. And Charles had dismissed the idea that the two men were disruptive to the office.

But one thing he was sure of – both he and Charles missed the presence of Mrs. Sullivan. Her humor and warmth, of course, but also her efficiency. Always doing the right thing for the business, whether it meant staying late or coming in on the weekends, and her talent for bringing out the best in others. He realized what a rare quality that was.

At any rate, when he had mentioned how much he missed Mrs. Sullivan, Charles had quickly agreed.

"She held everything together, and did so in a kindly manner. I do miss that." Charles had leaned back in his desk chair and frowned in resignation. "But she's retired. Happily so. Deservedly so."

They were both thinking the same thing, but didn't want to say it. Mason and Charles exchanged looks.

Then Mason tentatively made the suggestion. "I don't suppose she would consider coming back. Part-time?"

Charles had slowly considered the idea. "Even one day a week would make a difference." He gave it some more thought. "I suppose we could meet her for lunch. Over the holidays."

"Or sooner," offered Mason.

"Hmm." Charles held a pencil and flipped it from point to eraser, over and over. "Possibly broach the subject. Couldn't hurt."

Mason didn't want to lose the opportunity. "I know she'd be happy to have lunch with us."

Charles nodded. "As long as we don't pressure her. She would agree to work seven days if she thought we were suffering in any way because of her absence."

Mason had to laugh. "Indeed, she would. We'll be very diplomatic. If she's happy with the way things are now, we won't even bring it up."

And so, they had met for lunch. Mason now laughed as he recalled the delicacy with which they had danced around the matter, asking how she spent her days, how she and Brendan were spending their time, how the nieces and nephews were.

Mason had brought up the subject of work by mentioning his sister Claudia and how much she missed the WAVES, how she was finishing up with school, and then hoped to find a job.

"Good for her! Work is good for people," Mrs. Sullivan said emphatically. "I must admit that I miss it."

A spark of hope flickered in their eyes – and a look of caution from Charles to Mason, not to push the matter too quickly.

"But you enjoy the freedom you now have with Brendan," Charles said. "Your time is now entirely your own."

"Yes. That is nice." She leaned back to make room when the waiter refilled their coffee. She added a splash of milk, and took a sip. "Though, if truth be told, I often have more time on my hands than I know what to do with. And now with Brendan helping Guido in his business venture, I find that I quite miss my days at the office."

Charles stirred the milk in his coffee more than was necessary. Mason nervously brushed at the table cloth. And coughed. Now was their chance. What was Charles waiting for? He cleared his throat. When he looked up, he saw that Mrs. Sullivan was looking at them both with her eyebrows raised. In her old take-charge, no-nonsense manner she quipped:

"Well, are you going to ask me or do I have to invite myself back to work?"

And that was that. A schedule of three days a week was happily agreed on by all.

A few days had already passed, and Mrs. Sullivan was back on board and part of the crew, already injecting a much-missed oomph into the office atmosphere. Cheerful, witty, generous, and providing a comforting presence to the newly hired returning servicemen. With the exception of Eric and Bo, who were not happy about her role there. They felt it was a diminishment to their authority. But to everyone else, and especially to Mason and Charles, she was a welcome change.

Yes, Mason now thought, looking up and noticing signs of Christmas in the store windows, life was good. The war was over. Mrs. Sullivan was back at work. And three of his sisters were married! One more to go, and then he could truly relax for a change.

And the reason why his step was so brisk at this moment, was that the youngest sister, Alice, was on her way home for a visit with her husband, up from Fort Benning. He hadn't seen them since the wedding and was greatly looking forward to their visit.

He had seen Edith and Desmond over the summer when they came to visit, but he hadn't seen

Alice since the double wedding with Helen and her husband in February. Alice's husband, Matthew, had plans to leave the military and join his old work place, but that wouldn't happen until the spring. But it meant that she would be back in New York City. Alice, Helen, and Claudia all close by.

Mason had balked a little at the haste with which Alice and Helen had gotten married. But with the war over, everyone wanted to be married, have a home, start a family. Couldn't blame them.

Thankfully, Helen and her husband lived only a few blocks away, and Claudia was living at home again after her discharge from the WAVES. She would soon settle down and marry, surely.

He had hoped that Edith and Desmond might reconsider moving back to New York. That their visit might reawaken their love for the city. But for now, Hollywood suited them both. It was a good move for Desmond and he was succeeding as both an actor and a screenwriter, and Edith was working part-time as an editor of scripts.

He smiled again. Three of his four sisters were now home for Christmas. Yes, life was good. He had stopped off at the bakery on his way home to get some treats for his children – the Christmas cupcakes they so loved, and some cream puffs for his sisters. Alice always had a sweet tooth.

When he opened the door, still smiling in anticipation, no one noticed that he was home. The house was filled with laughter and talking and his kids running around. His wife, Susan, his mother, and his sisters Helen and Claudia were all gathered around Alice, laughing and talking all at once.

He hung up his coat and walked into the living room. "Daddy!" cried his youngest, running to him. He lifted his little girl and she excitedly pointed to the others. "Look! Aunt Alice is here!"

His eldest daughter, one of the twins, came to greet him as well. So like her mother, Mason thought as he handed her his five-year-old.

Alice spotted him and ran over with her arms outstretched. "Robert!"

"Hello, Alice!" Mason said, embracing her, and shaking her husband's hand. "Matthew! You both look well. Good to see you!"

After a flurry of greetings, his sister Helen cried out from the other side of the room, "I told you he wouldn't notice!"

Mason was used to being criticized for not noticing his sisters' clothes and hairstyles, and he promptly defended himself. "Of course I do. Alice is wearing her hair differently. Isn't she?" He looked at her hair but it seemed the same.

He was puzzled by the increased laughter, and exchanged a quick glance with his wife and mother, who were enjoying the scene.

"What? And getting a Georgia tan. I see it. I'm not blind. Looking more like Edith in that regard." There was more laughter. "Yes, yes, dressed in stylish clothes – " His eyes only then dropped down to her outfit and he noticed the roundness under her dress.

Mason's head snapped up and he looked from Alice to his wife, and back to Alice. Susan laughed and kissed him. "You're going to be an uncle!"

"An uncle?" He had to wonder at his surprise. Wasn't this the natural course of things? And yet, he had never thought of any of his sisters as mothers. A mother! Little Alice! He had to swallow the lump in his throat.

"Alice," he said, gently enfolding her in his arms.

"I'm so jealous!" cried Helen. "I was so sure *I* would be the first."

Alice laughed. "You'll be right on our heels, I'm sure."

"And then you, Claudia," said Helen.

Alice put a hand on her hip and turned to Claudia. "Are you engaged and didn't tell me?"

"No!" cried Claudia with a laugh. "That's just Helen trying to plan my life."

"Oh, pooh!" said Helen. "Don't listen to her. She's been seeing Philip Cooper for almost a year now. He adores her!"

"But she's finishing up with college and will get a job first," said Susan. "Which I think is a smart idea."

Alice rolled her eyes. "We all know how Claudia loves books and studying and – "

"And radio technology and frequency and other horrible sounding things," added Helen. "I can't even get her to go shopping with me. She'd rather talk about – electric magnets!"

Claudia gave a burst of laughter. "Electro-magnetism. And if I could get you to listen about it for five minutes, I'm sure you'd find it interesting."

"Fat chance! The war is over, Claudia. We don't have to be boring and practical anymore."

Alice perked up at that. "Oh, Helen, I want to go shopping soon. There's nothing like a New York City department store for glamour and fashion." She turned to Claudia. "And *you're* coming with us!"

"I'm busy that day," said Claudia, causing her sisters to laugh.

Their mother had been enjoying the sparring, but now spoke in a more serious tone. "You should go with them, Claudia." She gave her daughter a knowing nod. "If you're serious about finding a job, you'll need an interview suit."

"I plan on using my WAVES suit. It's extremely well made." She turned to her fashionable sisters. "Don't worry, I'll remove the insignia and wear a necklace or something."

"And what if there's a second interview?" questioned her mother.

"I'll wear a different blouse."

"Don't encourage her, mother." Mason tried not to frown at what he saw as Claudia's stubbornness. He had a latent fear that she would prove to be unreasonable and try to take a different path from the expected one.

"Don't worry, Robert," Alice said to her brother. "We'll have her engaged to Philip before I head back to Georgia."

"Fat chance!" said Claudia, in imitation of Helen.

Mason's mother spread her arms around her daughters, shepherding them into the dining room. "Come, come, girls, to the table! We can argue about all that later. Dinner is almost ready."

Susan came and kissed Mason's cheek. "How was your day, dear?"

Mason was grateful for his wife's tenderness and calm among his boisterous, spirited sisters. What would he do without her? He sniffed the air, and the aroma coming from the kitchen made him realize how hungry he was. He scooped up his little girl into his arms and gave her a kiss. Yes, he thought again as they followed the others into the dining room, life is good.

Chapter 4

In Lillian's kitchen, the scent of garlic and herbs filled the air as she stirred the marinara sauce on the stove. She was deep in thought about the morning's meeting at Haden Books – now Haden Publishing House. It had gone from being a small design firm, had expanded into books, and was now a full-blown publishing company. And they were busier than ever. Under Mrs. Huntington, Lillian had adjusted with the changing needs, working weekends, producing covers and illustrations for children's books and, increasingly, women's books and magazines.

With the end of war, the business had changed. It was more commercial now, driven by market demands. The women's book sector was exploding as women transitioned from wartime labor roles back to civilian life. They had more time, and their needs and interests were now different. All good for Haden Publishing, and, so far, working to her advantage, as well. There was more opportunity, more demand.

Lillian stopped stirring, and stared in thought. Besides all those changes, something was different in the office. She couldn't put her finger on it. She recalled the meeting, and the tone.

Ah, she thought, landing on the difference. It was something about Mrs. Huntington. She was quieter, more reserved.

Lillian shook some dried herbs into her palm and held them to her nose. Before crushing them between her fingers, she took a moment to enjoy the pungent scent of rosemary, the sweetness of the basil.

The meeting... Once again, she saw the table, ringed with the book design team. The attitude towards Mrs. Huntington seemed different, *that* was it. She wasn't being included as much in the discussions. She used to lead the meetings, and drove most of the decisions, though always with consensus.

But today? The few times she had made a point, there were merely nods, or vague responses from the group. No lively discussions as in the past. And Mr. Borland drove the meeting. He had been hired in the spring and had already been promoted twice. He was the nephew of one of the directors and was eager to prove himself.

Of course, the entire staff was different now. Lillian turned down the burner and gave the sauce a few more stirs. Many of the women had left – their husbands and fiancés had returned and they were now getting married and starting families, or, in the case of the older women, returning to their previous lives. The company was back to the way it used to be. Before the war.

But Lillian hadn't known the company before the war, and so, to her, it felt completely different. She missed the casual friendships she had grown accustomed to, the female banter, the support they all gave to each other through the difficult times. Fortunately, she still had Mrs. Huntington, and both their working relationship and their friendship had deepened over the past two years.

Lillian jumped when she felt Charles's arms around her. "Oh! I thought you were asleep on the couch."

Charles took a whiff of the sauce and smiled. "Just a cat nap."

"Mom! Charlotte needs changed," came Tommy's voice from the living room.

"I can stir this," said Charles, taking the spoon.

"Mom!" came Tommy's voice, this time more urgent.

Lillian handed Charles the spoon and turned the oven off. "And can you take out the garlic bread?"

She hurried away and whisked a crying Charlotte into the bedroom. After a few minutes, she returned to the kitchen with Charlotte happily babbling in her arms.

Charles reached out and lifted the toddler. "There's my big girl!" He sat at the table with her on his lap, bouncing her. "Oh – how was your meeting? Are we ready to celebrate?"

"Not quite yet. They seemed pleased with the preliminary designs. For the most part. I have to submit some changes. And they will give me a specific layout to follow. A formula, really."

Lillian drained the pasta, and added a few drops of olive oil. Then she poured the marinara sauce over it, tossed it, and poured it into a large earthenware bowl. Charles had forgotten to take out the garlic bread and it was burned around the edges. She frowned as she scraped off the worst parts, and arranged the slices on a platter. She set it next to the salad on the table, and then untied her apron and hung it inside the pantry door.

"Charles, do you notice a change in your office, now that things are back to normal? I mean now that most of the servicemen have refilled the jobs. Say, from a year ago."

He gave it some thought and shook his head. "No. For the most part, it feels like it did before the war. Especially now with Mrs. Sullivan back. Why do you ask?"

Lillian made a noncommittal sound and called Tommy and Gabriel in to dinner.

"Smells delicious!" cried Gabriel, taking his seat. Then he jumped up and pulled Charlotte's high chair next to the table.

"Tommy, can you bring the parmesan cheese? It's on the counter."

Charles followed up on her comment, as he put Charlotte in her high chair. "Did the meeting feel different today?"

"Oh, you know, I'm not there on a daily basis, but over the past few months – it just feels different." She scooted in her chair. "I think in large part because so many of the women have left, in management. Now it's just the secretaries, a few artists, and Mrs. Huntington. All the others are gone."

Gabriel held up his plate while Charles served him some pasta. "They went back home to have babies."

"Gabriel!" Lillian said in surprise.

"What? That's what they say at school."

Tommy glanced at Charles and hid his smile.

Lillian helped herself to some salad and handed the bowl to Tommy. "Well, yes. But that wasn't the reason. Many of them had to leave, to make room for the returning servicemen."

Tommy looked over at her. "But that was the right thing to do, wasn't it?"

"Of course," said Lillian. "They're finally back and they all need jobs. They risked their lives. Many have come back wounded. Everything must be done to help them."

"I've managed to hire most of the ones I had before the war," said Charles. "The ones who came back. Along with several new ones, though some of them are still settling in."

Lillian smiled to see the boys enjoying the meal. She fed Charlotte a spoon of chopped spaghetti, but Charlotte wanted the spoon to feed herself. "We're all happy things are getting back to normal."

"Not Mrs. Wilson, right Mom?" asked Gabriel, scraping off the burned edges of his garlic toast and then dipping it in the marinara sauce.

Charles raised his eyebrows at the comment. "What do you mean?"

"We passed her the other day. Gabriel thinks she misses her job."

"She'll adjust," said Charles. "Harry's glad to have her home. He said he enjoys having someone to come home to. There were many nights she had to work late and he had to make dinner himself! He's happy those days are over."

"Yes, that must be nice for him," Lillian replied.

Charles looked up, hearing a touch of sarcasm in her tone. "It's only natural. I love opening the door knowing that you and the boys are here to greet me. The sounds and smells of dinner being prepared."

Lillian gave a soft "hmm," but didn't respond.

"Mom wouldn't know about that, Dad," explained Gabriel. "Since she's the mom, you know."

Charles took another helping of pasta and sprinkled parmesan over it. "This is delicious." Then he made an attempt to soften his point. "It will take her some time, of course. Harry said she's taken to wandering around the apartment, cleaning out the same drawers and cupboards. Not used to having so much time on her hands."

"She has a lot of energy," Gabriel said, repeating Lillian's comment about Mrs. Wilson.

"Most women are only too happy to go back to the way things were," Charles said. "It's too bad her sons live upstate."

Lillian started to answer, then changed her mind.

"I know she loved her job," Charles said, puzzled by Lillian's apparent annoyance. "But that was a temporary measure. To help the war effort."

Tommy also caught the simmering tension and tried to ease it. "It's way better now, Mom. We read about it in one of Dad's books. For my report. Back in ancient Rome, the women were inferior to the men and couldn't do lots of things." He realized it didn't come out quite as he had intended and added, "But it was a whole lot worse in ancient Greece."

"Well, thank goodness that was a long time ago and things have changed!" The sharpness in her comment caused Tommy and Gabriel to look up at her, forks paused in their hands.

Lillian snapped a glance to them, then to Charles. "Charles! Did you just roll your eyes at me?"

"No! No," he responded playfully. "Just wondering if that's a crack in the ceiling."

Tommy and Gabriel laughed at his response.

Lillian raised her eyebrows, and also responded playfully. "I think I'm outnumbered."

"Don't worry, Mom," said Gabriel, twirling some pasta. "Charlotte will be older soon. She'll be on your side. I'll be in the middle. Then it will be even."

Tommy looked up defensively. "I'm not taking sides! I just said that about Rome. It's in the book, for my report."

"And I was just pointing out what Harry said," Charles added, still with a smile playing about his mouth.

Lillian laughed at their excuses. "Oh, I know, I know. I'm not saying it's not all true." She leaned forward and spoke directly to Charles. "And believe me, I know how lucky I am."

He gave her a look of love, and took another helping of salad. "How's Izzy?" he asked, in a not-so-subtle attempt to change the subject.

"I'll find out tomorrow – I'm meeting her for lunch." As she told him their plans, she noticed that Gabriel was peering off in concentration.

"What are you so deep in thought about, Gabriel?"

"Ancient Rome."

"You too?" asked Lillian.

"For school. I have an idea for our ten-minute skit and I was just thinking about it."

"Have you decided on the topic?" asked Charles.

"Not quite. We still have two more days. If it's good enough, we'll be the grand finale. They always give it to the older students. That's us, now."

"What's your idea?" asked Lillian.

"I was thinking about those babies Dad was telling us about. Those twin brothers – Romie and Remie?"

"Romulus and Remus," Tommy corrected.

"But I figure they probably would have called each other Romie and Remie."

Tommy gave an exasperated look to Charles, who lightly shook his head and suppressed a smile. Then to Lillian, Tommy said, "They founded Rome. According to mythology."

"I know," said Lillian. "I did an illustration for that. Two babies nursed by a she-wolf." She suddenly grew concerned at the possibilities in Gabriel's idea. "But how would you use that in a skit?"

She saw that Tommy had stopped chewing and also appeared worried.

Charles chuckled and asked, "What do you have in mind, Gabriel?"

Still peering into the distance, Gabriel fanned open his hands in a dramatic fashion. The table grew quiet. "In the darkness you hear two babies crying. The lights slowly come on and there you see it – the baby brothers nursing at the she-wolf."

Tommy jerked back in his seat. "How are you going to show that?"

"I got it all figured out. Me and Billy will be the babies. We'll make a cutout of the wolf really big so that we look small."

Lillian's concern increased as she imagined the scene: two good-sized boys, twelve and thirteen – in diapers? Arms and legs kicking under a large she-wolf. She thought of Billy's love of sound effects and imagined loud gurgling, crying – surely, he wouldn't make sucking sounds?

Tommy put his fork down. "How is that patriotic? That's the theme," he explained helplessly to Charles.

Gabriel gave it some thought. "It's Italian patriotic," he replied, and took a bite of pasta.

Tommy groaned in exasperation. "That's not what they're talking about, Gabriel."

Gabriel pondered this, tipped his head left, right, then he held up his fork. "I've got it. An easy fix. The final scene will show how the Italians eventually immigrated to New York City! And fought in the war."

"That's a lot of history to cover in ten minutes," said Lillian.

Gabriel looked at all three doubting faces. "Maybe it's too much. That was just one idea. I have some others."

Tommy let out a sigh of relief and soon Lillian was waving them into the living room. "I'll clean up here."

Tommy lifted Charlotte, and washed her hands and face at the sink. He and Gabriel played with her and her stuffed animals on the living room rug, laughing as they asked her to make different animal sounds.

"Her horse sounds just like a sheep!" said Tommy.

After the kitchen was tidied, Lillian came into the living room and set a few plates on the coffee table. "The last of Mrs. Kuntzman's Thanksgiving pecan pie."

Gabriel continued his train of thought. "I'll find a better idea. I didn't like Romulus killing Remus, anyway. Like Cain and Abel. What's wrong with these famous brothers? Why can't they be friends? Like me and Tommy? I mean Tom." He grinned and punched Tommy on the arm.

Without looking at him, Tommy's arm pivoted out at the elbow and smacked Gabriel on the chest. They were soon wrestling on the floor, laughing and thoroughly enjoying themselves.

"Boys! Boys! Stop that right now!" cried Lillian. Even Charlotte was whooping with merriment. "What kind of example are you setting for your sister? Charles!"

Charles walked over as if to break them up, but instead grabbed the pillow from Gabriel and threw it at Lillian.

"Oh, yes?" She took a larger pillow from the couch and hit Charles with it, just as he pulled her onto the couch, both of them laughing in the tussle.

Charlotte jumped into the fray, falling spread-eagle on top of Tommy and Gabriel, and letting out a gurgling scream of delight.

"I think she's going to be a fighter, Mom!" said Gabriel

"Let's hope so," Lillian said, dodging another pillow from Charles.

Chapter 5

After Lillian and Izzy embraced and exclaimed how it couldn't possibly be three months since they last saw each other, they briefly caught up on the superficial facts of their lives as they perused the menu. They then placed their orders, and settled more comfortably into the restaurant booth.

Izzy convinced Lillian to join her with a French 75 and raised her glass to Lillian when the drinks arrived.

"Such an evocative name." Lillian took a sip and mused on the crisp, citrusy drink. "What do you think it refers to – perhaps the address of a mysterious assignation." She envisioned the Paris skyline, a mansard roof with golden light spilling onto a balcony…

"I think it's a World War One drink," said Izzy, enjoying the flavors.

"Oh." Lillian revised the image. "Maybe it involved a spy. Or an actress who –"

"You're such a romantic. It was a French field gun," said Izzy, laughing at Lillian's disappointment. "A cannon. Explains the kick," she said, flicking the rim of her glass and making it ring. "So," she said, folding her arms on the table, "you said you're still at the hospital? I thought Artists for Victory wrapped up earlier in the year."

"It did, officially. I still teach one night a week, but I expect that to end after the holidays. Once in a while Gabriel comes and helps Henry in the rec room. But even that is winding down. Most of the volunteers, including Henry, now go to the VA hospitals."

"The volunteers," echoed Izzy, remembering the past. "You know, sometimes I think back to those years and I wonder how I ever found the energy. To volunteer most nights, after a full day at work. Often dancing at the Stage Door Canteen! I'm not sure I could still do it."

"And weekends! You were unstoppable, Izzy. Always ready to take on more."

"We were all that way." Izzy gave a small laugh at that earlier version of herself. "Everything is different now, isn't it? In a good way," she was quick to add. She glanced around at the pine boughs and ornaments decorating the restaurant arches. "And now Christmas is upon us, once again."

"As the boys keep reminding us. We got our tree and have decorated the new place. It's our first Christmas there, so we went all out. We made a day of it – getting a tree and wreaths, bunches of holly, and going out for dinner afterwards. While the boys and Charles decorated the tree, I finished up on my fruit cake." She handed Izzy a Christmas tin, heavy with the annual holiday loaf. "For you and Red."

Izzy opened the tin and smiled. "Our favorite Christmas dessert. Red will be delighted. That reminds me," she said, rummaging in her tote. She slid an envelope across to Lillian. "For your baking."

Lillian peeked inside and saw the sugar rationing coupons. "Are you sure, Izzy? Thank you!" She tucked them inside her purse. "I've been wanting to get started on my Christmas cookies."

"And – " Izzy took out a small paper bag and handed it to Lillian. "I was browsing through Gimbles and came across these."

Lillian lifted out a box of shimmering glass ornaments. "Oh, Izzy, they're beautiful!" She lifted out a pale pink and blue ball with silver glitter decorating the crescent moons and shooting stars.

"That one caught my eye. It made me think of Charlotte. And the brighter red and blue ones for the boys. There was a crowd around them – everyone wants glass ornaments, now that they're fully available again."

"Imported?" Lillian asked, admiring the delicate globe as she held it up to the light.

Izzy laughed and tapped the box. "Yes, from New Jersey. Shiny Brite. Proper ornaments this year – silvered inside, and wire hooks. No more cardboard caps or strings on top."

"They're exquisite, Izzy. The kids will be thrilled." She gently set the box in the bag and tapped it. "We'll hang them tonight. You'll have to stop by and see our tree."

"Now that I'm not working Saturdays, I'll be able to find the time."

Lillian waited to see if Izzy would say anything more about her decision. "So, you're sure about leaving the construction company? You were seriously considering working full time at one point, weren't you?"

Izzy looked off and twisted her mouth. "It was a bad idea from the beginning. I thought – initially, I thought it would help to be close to Red, where I could keep an eye on him." She gazed out the window and spoke in a subdued voice. "He has lows, you know. The doctor says it will diminish with time. That it's not unusual for returning servicemen." She then explained how Red had met up with one of his crew members. "But now that Joe Sanchez will be working with Red, I won't have to worry. He'll be there for Red. He'll understand his moods in a way that his family can't."

"It sounds like the perfect solution. And you can stay at Rockwell."

They smiled at the waiter who set down bowls of cream of mushroom soup.

"Mmm. Looks delicious. Perfect for a cold day."

They enjoyed a few spoonfuls of soup. "I'll have to try making this for Charles and the boys. I think they'd enjoy it."

Izzy's thoughts were still on her job. "I can't tell you how relieved I am. And I can stop tormenting myself about whether I should leave Rockwell. I'll work for another five, ten years or so, see where life takes us then."

"Good. I'm glad you can keep your job. I know how much it means to you."

Izzy buttered a roll to eat with her soup. "Red wants to buy a house. I told him I have a chunk saved, but he doesn't want me to touch it. The Protector. The Provider. But I never needed one or had one. I go along with him, for the most part."

Lillian smiled at Izzy's comment. She knew that Izzy was a savvy saver and had managed her money well over the years. She also knew that she would defer to Red on anything that would help to bring him some peace.

"His father is pressuring him to build a big house in the suburbs, close to his brothers." Izzy lifted her glass, and then set it down. "Honestly? I'm just grateful that I don't have to change jobs. Life has been too full of changes for too long. I don't want any more. I told Red we could think about a house later. My apartment is perfect for us, for now."

They leaned back as their soup bowls were cleared and their main courses were placed before them. "I know what you mean. I feel like I've finally earned the job of my dreams, and I don't want any more changes."

Izzy raised her glass. "To no more changes!" She emptied the last of her drink, but held the glass as she set it down. "But it's not the same, is it? Work. Besides you not being at Rockwell Publishing, many of the other women are gone now."

Lillian took a sip of her drink, and agreed with Izzy. "It's the same with my job. A lot of new people. Or old employees returning. But my job itself is pretty much the same. Do you feel that yours is different?" she asked, finishing her drink.

"Oh, yes," Izzy said lightly. "I've been stripped of my authority. At least it feels that way. I used to do the work of two, three people. And I loved it." She twisted her glass around and again looked out the window. "Of course, it benefitted me too. I needed to stay busy. To keep me from worrying about Red. Especially after he was injured. And then…afterwards, you know." Izzy rubbed her face. "Those were hard times. Thank God, they're over." She cut into her filet mignon and made a sound of enjoyment. Then she speared a chunk of roasted potato. "And yet at times, they were also exhilarating."

"They were charged times," said Lillian. "I think the fear and uncertainty heightened everything. I'm so glad it's behind us. And yet I know what you mean." She sampled her Coquilles Saint-Jacques and savored the delicate flavors. "Delicious!"

A sudden surge of nostalgia filled Izzy, along with a desperate yearning for – she didn't even know what. She snagged the waiter as he walked by. "Two glasses of champagne!" She leaned forward towards Lillian. "For old times' sake!"

As the waiter cleared their old glasses, Lillian gave a laugh at Izzy's exuberance. She realized how much she missed seeing her old friend on a regular basis. She needed Izzy in her life, and promised herself that she would see more of her.

They were soon sipping champagne, searching for the effervescence of former times in the golden bubbly.

"To our days at Rockwell Publishing!" Lillian said. "We had some swell times."

They reminisced over a few incidents, and Lillian recounted her slow but sure progress as an artist. "I still can't believe it. And I have you to thank for it, Izzy, for helping me to get hired at Rockwell Publishing. That's where it really all began."

"I knew it was the right step for you. Plus, I selfishly wanted you there."

"It's so important to have an ally, isn't it? As much as I love my work, I think it's the guidance and friendship with Mrs. Huntington that most matters to me. As well as with many of the others. I was really sorry to see some of them go."

"I know what you mean. Some of the gals were furious when Rockwell let them go. Forced them out, really. But it was to be expected. And of course, we're back to no mothers or expecting women working. Some are trying to hide their pregnancies for as long as possible. They need their jobs."

"What about your friend at the shipyard? Maureen?"

"She got her pink slip months ago. Along with the other women. She told me that most of the men had come round to accepting them – after all the push back, and oftentimes, outright hostility, they had to put up with in the beginning. Though there were plenty who were happy to see them go. A few even cheered."

"That's a shame."

They sipped on their champagne, and were quiet for a few moments. Then Lillian added, "Though, again, it was to be expected. The returning men must have work."

"Yes, of course." Izzy's eyes narrowed in thought as she twisted her glass around. "There's a lot of resentment out there. Women gave it their all during the war. Were asked to take jobs they never would have dreamed of taking – welders, riveters, munitions work, crane operators! Good God, they did it all! Worked late hours, weekends... Now, they're being told to go home. They're no longer needed."

Lillian thought of Mrs. Wilson and almost told Izzy about her plight, but decided against it. She wanted their lunch to be cheerful.

Izzy seemed to think the same thing. "And you?" she asked brightly, cutting into her filet again. "Your work is going well? Let me tell you, we are the lucky ones."

"Yes, we are. I certainly feel that way." Lillian took another of the scallops arranged on her plate. "Though..."

"What?"

"The atmosphere is different. Mrs. Huntington is pretty much the only woman in management now. And there are fewer women artists. At the latest meeting it was announced that Mrs. Huntington will now report to Mr. Borland, the new director. I'm not sure what it means, but I don't see how it can be viewed as anything but a demotion. He's taking her office. She'll be out with the secretaries now." Lillian slowly shook her head as she remembered the meeting. "I kept wondering why she wasn't speaking up. She didn't show much emotion, but she clearly wasn't happy."

"She probably understood that it would be pointless." Izzy leaned her head in thought. "She's been there a long time, hasn't she?"

"Almost from the beginning. She helped establish the department, over ten years ago. Under her management the book department flourished."

"And how is he, this Mr. Borland? Do you think you'll enjoy working with him?"

"I don't know. He seems to like my work. He described the series of books in fuller detail – though it was originally Mrs. Huntington's idea."

"The women in the workforce series. Sounds interesting."

"I'm so excited about it. I can't wait to begin on the covers." Her enthusiasm slowly gave way to a quiet tension, and she began absentmindedly pushing the creamed spinach around her plate. "When he speaks about it, it's as if it was all his idea. I've noticed that he has a way of taking credit for deals that have already been made. For past successes that belong to Mrs. Huntington."

Izzy let out a deep sigh. "I'm familiar with the pattern. I'd say Mrs. Huntington has an uphill battle. Not without someone there to champion her. Past actions are in the past. This new guy will steamroll right over her."

"Which most likely means the same will happen to me. I'm her 'find,' after all. She brought me in."

"But they're happy with your work, aren't they? If your covers help sales, they'll keep you. It's as simple as that. The ole bottom line." Izzy took another sip of champagne, which had lost its cold crispness.

"I submitted several drawings for the covers, as a first step. The only initial requirement was that they focus on love, marriage, and beauty. After years of working with Rockwell, I was already well aware of marketing strategies."

"So, it's a done deal? They liked your drawings?"

Lillian nodded hesitantly, and took a sip of champagne. "They liked them. But there are some very specific changes they want me to make."

Izzy cocked her head. "Such as?"

"The team made vague suggestions, such as, 'the face is right, but the figure needs some attention. More curves, perhaps a hip jutting out to one side. And make sure the male figure is above the female. Larger. With the woman looking up to him.' That kind of thing. Even though the story is about a successful woman architect. 'Give her a gentler look, less determination.' They confirmed everything with nods from Mr. Borland. I guess he knows what will sell."

"He sounds like Rockwell."

Lillian lifted and dropped her shoulders in resignation. "Mrs. Huntington and I are going to meet after work sometime next week. The way she spoke – I had the strangest feeling that we shouldn't be seen speaking together. It was a new feeling, very uncomfortable."

A heavy silence hung between them. "I'm sorry to hear that. It sounds to me like the old jockeying for power. He must see her as a threat. But the artists shouldn't be affected by it."

"No. I suppose not. But enough of all that," Lillian said, with a wave of her hand. "How's Lois? Any plans to visit her over the holidays?"

"Of course! She's coming up in two weeks to do some Christmas shopping. She can't wait to see all the latest fashions. No more restrictions with hems and trim. Everything is available now." Izzy's fork sat in her hand. "It's funny…"

Lillian looked up and waited for her to finish her thought.

"After years of restrictions and 'make it do or do without,' hammered into us, I find the idea of splurging a little difficult. It seems indulgent. Selfish. We took such pride in making do." She gave a guilty smile. "Lois told me I'll get over that pretty quickly."

"I'm sure your sister's right," said Lillian. "The displays I've seen in the department store windows are very enticing, I have to say. Richer fabrics, beautiful lines, so many choices."

"Almost overwhelming," Izzy said with a laugh. "Though, I think it's different for Red. He doesn't say much, but I think he finds all this buying very jarring. After years of deprivation and knowing what it's like over there." She gave a nod indicating the direction of Europe.

Lillian tipped her head, wondering what she meant.

"We were walking down Fifth Avenue the other day, looking at the window displays. You know me, a pretty dress always cheered me up. So, I paused in front of a window, amused at the heavy-handed emphasis on glamour in the kitchen. There was a mannequin in a beautiful dress and – get this – the apron she was wearing was trimmed in sequins! And she was holding matching potholders. A little over-the-top, perhaps, but they're sure to sell. Along with the enamel stoves and refrigerators. And chrome toasters and percolators and egg timers and ice crushers." Izzy shook her head at the vision. "And in the middle of it all, the new domestic goddess. Sequined. I looked over at Red and he just stared at it all, saying, 'It's too much. It's all just too much.'"

As Lillian envisioned Red and his response, it seemed familiar. "It sounds like one of the soldiers Gabriel has befriended. Someone from the hospital. He can't be around loud noises and crowds and shoppers. He's taken refuge in the park. Says the hospital did all they can for him. Now he just wants to be left alone."

Izzy nodded slowly as she took this in. "I can imagine how unsettling it must be for them. The contrast. I've notice that Red's a little more at ease in the Village. It's quieter. Not so bright. He likes to go to the coffee houses and pubs there. He said people there talk about things that matter."

Once again, they both became aware of the conversation slipping into the worrisome.

Izzy finished her now warm, flat champagne and put on a happy face. "And how's your sister Annette? And what do you hear from Charles's sister Kate?"

"Both doing extremely well."

"I imagine things are pretty much the same for them. I mean, they were working long before the war even started."

Lillian took a bite of the scallops and nodded. "Annette and Bernie could barely keep up with the demand this year, they were so busy with the orchard. And Kate is still busy with the farm, but without the pressure. Her sons have pretty much settled in. All married now. Starting their families."

"Kate must be in heaven. And the wives? You met them all, over the summer, didn't you?"

"Yes, and loved them. All three of them." Lillian finished her champagne and pushed the glass aside. "Though in Kate's last letter, she did mention some tension between Edna and Eugene, the eldest son."

"Edna's the nurse, right?"

"Yes. She still wants to work and Eugene can't understand it. Now that she doesn't have to. Gladys, Jimmy's wife, on the other hand, was only too happy to give up her job at the dry goods store. And Paul's wife, Lucille, still works at the library, though not as often. I'm not sure why."

Izzy gave a general smile. "I guess everyone is adjusting. Mr. Rockwell is happy, I can tell you that. The economy is booming and the business is making money. He's pushing us all to keep up with the changes. At our latest advertising meeting, there was emphasis on the abundance of choices – fashions, the new appliances, all the cosmetics and lotions, and steering women into wanting. 'Create desire,' he said." Izzy stared down at the table cloth, a crease forming between her brows. "Sometimes, you get the feeling that we're all just puppets being told what to buy, what to want, what to do. Go home and have babies! Get married and buy a house and fill it with new merchandise. With sequins."

"Oh, Izzy," laughed Lillian. "It's not so grim as all that. I think people just want to be happy after the dark years. There's a feeling of hope, and prosperity is a part of it. Don't you think?"

"I guess so." She began to lift her glass then remembered it was empty.

"There's a similar drive for books. They say the market will be booming now that so many women are out of the workforce. They'll have time to read more, which is a good thing. Though I'm glad I'll be depicting women in jobs. The challenge is greater, and I find it so inspiring."

Izzy suddenly thought of something. "Remember Louisa from the Art Department?"

"Of course. So talented. I learned a lot from her."

"She came up with an ad you would have loved. Of a very stylish woman in a suit, stepping into the driver's seat of *her* car! No prince charming opening the passenger door for her. Very smart. The head of the art department praised it at a meeting."

"I like it. That would make a good book cover," she said, mentally adding it to her store of images.

"Of course, he then reminded her that the focus now is on the domestic and to add a beautiful house in the background. He said that women are only too happy to return to their traditional roles and they want to buy, buy, buy!" Izzy did a quick impersonation of him. "'Just as you glamorized war work, you will now glamorize housework. It's patriotic, it's healthy, and it's back to normal!' Izzy groaned. "He sounded like a slogan. And he actually threw his fist in enthusiasm as he said it."

Lillian gave a weak smile. "I can just hear him saying that. Back to normal." She sat back as the waiter cleared their plates.

Then, in an overly cheerful tone, she added, "Though it won't feel like it's back to normal until the sugar ration is finally lifted."

"That will surely happen soon! Though not in time for all your Christmas baking."

And the conversation was steered into the safer waters of the coming holiday season.

Chapter 6

During a lull in business at the Red String, Gabriel and Mr. G stood at the counter while Henry and Dusty debated whether the new television craze would last or fizzle away.

"You can't get near the displays in the windows, the crowds are so thick around them," said Henry.

"All to see a little box with a flickering picture. Can't see the allure," said Dusty.

Gabriel's after-school shifts always flew by much too quickly for him, but he glanced at the clock and decided that he had just enough time. "Mr. G," he asked, "do you mind if I go check on my friend? It won't take long."

"Your veteran friend? Not at all. And let me treat you both to a cup of hot chocolate." He opened the till and gave Gabriel a few coins. "We can't do enough for our veterans. Far too many of them without – well, get him a hot chocolate from me, and tell him to stop by. At least it's warm in here."

"Thanks! He might not even be there. But if he is, that will make him real happy. Happy! Did I tell you that's his name? Short for Harrison. And even shorter, Hap."

"Yes, you did. And is he a happy fellow?"

Gabriel shook his head. "No. He says his name is short for hapless."

"Bring him in sometime. That might cheer him up."

"I'll ask him, but he doesn't like to be around people, especially shoppers. That's why he goes to the park." Gabriel pulled on his coat and ran out the door. "I'll be back in a jiffy!"

Gabriel went to his favorite vendor in Central Park, the one who added free marshmallows to the hot chocolate. Then he went to the bench near the pond where he often saw Hap.

"Hap!" He waved as he hollered out to him, glad that he was there today. "A present from Mr. G. Hot chocolate! One for you," he said, handing him a cup, "and one for me. He wants you to stop by. You should. I think you'd like his company."

"Thanks, Gabriel. Tell him thanks from me." He took a moment to warm his hands around the cup, then took a sip and nodded that it was good.

"No work today?"

Hap shook his head. "I didn't go. Maybe I'll check the boards tomorrow. See if there's something for me."

Gabriel knew that most jobs didn't suit Hap. "Did you like working as a night guard? That must have been quiet."

"That wasn't bad. Might do that again."

"My mom remembers you from last year. She says hi. She asked if your leg was all healed now." Gabriel took off the lid to his hot chocolate to get at the melting marshmallows.

"The leg's good. The problem, they tell me, is nerves. Can't take too much." They sipped on their hot chocolate and watched as a duck streaked onto the pond.

Gabriel smiled. "That looked nice, didn't it? The way he landed like that, making those long ripples."

Hap's face softened in pleasure. "Sure did. Real nice. Sometimes, I think – "

"What?"

"I got a brother. Upstate. He thinks I should go live there with him and his family."

"Why don't you?"

Hap turned suddenly and snapped at Gabriel. "It's none of his damned business what I do! I just want to be left alone."

From volunteering at the hospital, Gabriel had seen occasional outbursts in the men before and knew that it was best to ignore them. He continued to watch the ducks as he drank his hot chocolate.

Hap rubbed his face and ran a hand through his hair. Then he pulled on his beard. "The problem is, I got combat fatigue, Gabriel. You know what that is?"

Gabriel raised his eyebrows as he gave it some thought. "I guess it means you're tired of fighting."

Hap gave a long laugh and slapped Gabriel on the back. "That's exactly what it means. Sick and tired of it all."

Gabriel tipped his cup over his mouth and tapped at the bottom to get the remaining sweetness. "Well, I gotta go, Hap."

"Be seeing you, Gabriel." Hap lifted his cup. "Tell your boss thanks."

Gabriel darted through the park and was back in the shop just as the after-work crowd began to trickle in. He was soon helping a customer decide between several items for her Oriental Garden, as she referred to one corner of her tiny living room.

*

Lillian decided to meet Gabriel as he got off work at the Red String Curio Store, as she sometimes did, now that Charlotte was older. She left her sleeping peacefully under the watchful eyes of Tommy. Christmas was fast approaching and she needed to start her search for a few presents for Charles.

Recently, he had unboxed some of his old books in order to help Tommy with his school project. Since then, Lillian had sometimes come across Charles deeply engrossed in reading. He had even cleared a shelf in the bookcase for his old history books and novels. It was as if he was reclaiming, or perhaps rediscovering, his younger self.

He once told her that he had found solace in the wisdom of Marcus Aurelius and Cicero, so she was now scanning a shelf of books holding Greek and Roman philosophy, history, and drama.

Not finding anything that felt right, she turned to the shelves next to it full of novels. She pulled out a few of the Russian books and gazed at the covers of Tolstoy and Dostoyevsky. To her lighter-craving spirit, they seemed heavy and ponderous.

And yet, she remembered how moved she had been by the beauty and depth of *Anna Karinina* and *The Brothers Karamazov*. And George Eliot, one of her favorite authors, was also rather ponderous, wasn't she? And yet she was drawn to her novels.

But now? Perhaps it was the long, dark war years, and the bad news that was still pouring in about past – and current – events. She longed for something brighter and uplifting. Surely, Charles would feel the same way, wouldn't he?

She ran her fingers over Jane Austen and a smile came to her lips on seeing *Emma* and *Sense and Sensibility*. And then Dickens, of course, would make him smile – in between the darker parts. Hmm. Sir Athur Conan Doyle. Sure to be both entertaining and stimulating. Can't go wrong with Sherlock Holmes. She pulled out a few slim books and perused the ones in good shape. Charles might enjoy these. The cover illustrations alone made her smile – so dramatic. These were safe. She would get a few of these now and come back later to look more closely through the philosophy and history books.

Gabriel rounded the aisle, pencil behind his ear, a Chinese porcelain pagoda in his hands. "I'm almost ready Mom. Just returning this. What'd you find?"

Lillian showed him the covers. "What do you think of these? For your father?"

Gabriel's face lit up at her choice. "Everybody likes Sherlock. *The Hound of the Baskervilles* – I couldn't put it down. Sometimes I'll see a really big dog somewhere and I remember the story and get goosebumps. Wish I could figure things out like Sherlock."

Lillian laughed at his comment and realized that Gabriel was fast growing up. She would have to rethink some of the ideas she had in mind for his presents. "Good. It's a start. I'll just go and pay for these."

Gabriel set the pagoda among a few Chinese ginger jars, and reached for the books. "I'll carry them for you."

While at the counter, she chatted a bit with Mr. G, Dusty, and Junior. She had gotten to know them better over the past year and found them all quite knowledgeable and entertaining in their own unique manner. On seeing her choices, they began a discussion of their favorite Sherlock Holmes stories.

Dusty, seated at the checkers table with Junior, steepled his fingertips and tapped them together. "Interesting fact. Though associated with Sherlock, the phrase 'the game's afoot' was actually first used by Shakespeare. *Henry V.*"

"What game was that, Dusty?" Gabriel asked, taking off his green shop apron and hanging it on a peg behind the counter.

Junior rubbed his knees and said, "What else, but war with France? War," he grumbled. "Man's favorite game. Can't seem to get enough of it."

Dusty raised his hand, ready to expound on that claim. "Well now, in the case of King Henry –" when the front door burst open, the little bell jingled, and Billy came running in.

"Gabriel! There you are! I was afraid you were gone."

"Zounds!" cried Dusty. "You enter like a tempest!"

Mr. G chuckled. "The urgency of youth. A wonderful quality."

Billy stopped a moment and grew serious. He tapped his cheek. "Billy Tempest. Might make a good stage name."

"Hello, Billy!" said Lillian. "We're just about to leave. You can walk with us."

While Mr. G wrapped the Sherlock Holmes books, Billy greeted the others, and then came to the counter.

Gabriel was putting on his coat and then lifted the bundle of books tied with brown paper and red string.

"Glad you stopped by, Billy. We only have a few more days to hand in our idea. I have a couple of ideas that – "

"Sure, sure." In a lower voice, Billy added, "But there's something else we need to discuss first. Something else related to my – career." Billy raised and lowered his head in a mysterious manner. He made a series of gestures, hinting at something, and pointed his head towards the door.

Gabriel's eyebrows pinched in puzzlement as Billy ran his finger up and down the side of his nose and gave a slow nod. Gabriel tried to remember where he had seen those gestures – in a movie?

Billy glanced around, raised his eyebrows up and down, and gave another nod to the door.

"Is everything all right, Billy?"

"Is it ever." He gave a wink, a smile, and folded his arms importantly on his puffed-out chest.

"What? What is it?"

Billy looked around and saw that the others were all talking about books, so he leaned in and said, "Business." He rubbed his fingers together in another familiar gesture, maybe from the same movie. Was it about gangsters?

"Oh!" cried Gabriel. "I get it. Money."

Billy tapped the side of his nose again, and then ran his finger across it, then under it, then decided that was enough nose gestures. "I have to show you something. Right away."

Gabriel turned to Lillian. "Can I go to Billy's for a few minutes?"

"Of course." Lillian took the bundle of books from him. "But don't be late for dinner."

"I won't. Bye, Mr. G! Bye, Junior. See you later, Dusty!"

Billy pivoted on his heels, grabbed Gabriel's arm, and ran towards the door – bumping into Mrs. Wilson, who was just coming in.

"Oops, sorry!" he cried. He mock-gallantly held the door open for her and waved her inside.

"Hi, Mrs. Wilson," said Gabriel. "Any luck?"

Billy pulled him out of the store before she could answer.

Mrs. Wilson gave a laugh at the boys and walked up to Lillian. "I saw you from outside." She turned to the others. "Afternoon, gentlemen."

"Ah, Mrs. Wilson," said Mr. G. "The collection you inquired after will arrive on Thursday. In pristine condition. I'm sure Harry will be delighted."

"Can you wrap it? I don't trust him not to peek."

"Of course, of course," he said with a happy grin. "We're all like children when it comes to Christmas presents."

"For his stamp collection," Mrs. Wilson explained to Lillian. "Just leaving? I'll walk with you."

Lillian held up her package. "And I just picked up some books for Charles, for under the tree."

They said their goodbyes and left the Red String Curio Store. Lillian took a moment to admire the Christmas window Mr. G and Gabriel had worked on. "Looks very festive, doesn't it?"

"It certainly does." Mrs. Wilson leaned forward and took a closer look at the arrangement of toys and dolls, red and green glassware – and an odd assortment of mounted fish, on plaques and pieces of driftwood. "Interesting," she said, clearly amused.

Lillian laughed. "Most likely Gabriel's touch. What did he mean by 'any luck' – with what?"

Mrs. Wilson's smile instantly dropped, replaced by anger. She gave an indignant huff.

"I've been – job hunting. Thought I'd apply at a few places."

"Oh, I didn't know. Any chance of you going back to your job with the city?"

"Ha! None at all. They don't need us women now that the men are back. Plain and simple."

"Oh well, yes, that was to be expected. Where have you been applying?"

"Here and there." She gave another "humph" and shot an angry glance down the street. "The last place told me all their positions were filled. When I began to explain my qualifications, he cut me short and said the returning soldiers had first priority. That it was 'unseemly and unpatriotic' of me, an 'older lady,' to try to take their jobs away from them. *Unpatriotic!* Me!" She pulled her headscarf tighter under her chin – too tight in her anger. She whipped it off her head, repositioned it, and tied it more calmly. "Me!"

"Well, he clearly doesn't know you or he would never have suggested such a thing."

"He was so rude to me."

Lillian saw that Mrs. Wilson was blinking hard, as if to keep her tears in check. "Mrs. Wilson, no one worked harder than you in support of the war effort. My goodness, the bomb shelter, the countless drives, helping Harry and the others in their plane spotting, knitting! The countless caps and scarves you knitted for Bundles for Bluejackets, not to mention the bandages you rolled –"

Mrs. Wilson put a hankie to her nose and stuffed it back in her pocket. "Oh, plenty of people worked harder than I did. I know you're just trying to cheer me up." She gave Lillian's arm a squeeze. "I'm fooling myself. I won't find work. I do understand. Of course, I do. At my old job, my position has gone to a man who worked there before the war. Then he served. Was wounded. Twice! By the grace of God, he came back alive. Of course, he should have his job back. Of course! They all should. It's just that – " Her words hung in the air, unspoken.

They crossed onto the avenue, its sidewalk crowded now with people rushing home from work.

"It must be hard," said Lillian. "I know how much you loved your job."

"I loved everything about it!" Mrs. Wilson peered out over the busy sidewalk, dense with hurrying people, and gave a wistful smile. "That sense of purpose, that rushing along with everyone else. Yes, it could be grueling, exhausting, frustrating – but I loved it. I really did. I loved being a part of" – she swept her arm out – "all that."

Lillian looked out at the crowded sidewalk, the noisy traffic, the energetic rush-hour bustle, and understood the feeling. She placed a gentle hand on Mrs. Wilson's arm.

Mrs. Wilson looked almost sheepish for a moment. "I felt young again, like anything was possible. Now – I feel my years. The old aches and pains are surfacing once more." She gave a laugh. "Maybe I was just too busy to feel them before. I think it's good for the body and the mind to get up and get going. Push yourself a little. See what you're capable of."

"I completely agree," said Lillian. "I had that same abundance of energy during the war years. In large part, because I had to. I remember being surprised at how much I was able to accomplish."

Mrs. Wilson gave a sidelong look to Lillian. "And let me tell you another thing I miss – my paycheck! It was the only time in my life I got paid for work and that was a good feeling. I'll never forget my first paycheck. I just stared at it. My name on it."

Lillian smiled at the comment. "I remember my first paycheck at the department store. It changed how I saw myself. I felt more – capable. It's hard to explain."

Mrs. Wilson agreed, and they remained silent for a few moments, lost in their thoughts. "Sometimes, when I remember, I feel guilty. That while a war was raging, I was happy. I loved my job. I loved my team."

"You shouldn't feel that way. Your work was vital. Who knows what good you did, what lives were saved. Working women made it possible for more men to fight."

Mrs. Wilson forced a smile. "Thanks for trying to make me feel better. I know I did the right thing. Working when they needed me. Stepping aside when they didn't. Feels like motherhood all over again," she added with a laugh. "Raised my sons and then they left. As it should be. It's all as it should be."

Lillian didn't want to think about that time in the future. She couldn't imagine life without her children. She worried that they would move far from her. Or worse, that another war would take them away –

"But the fact remains – I miss my job." Mrs. Wilson thrust her hands into her coat pockets. "Oh, I'm not alone. There are lots of us. Ashamed to admit it. Some are fighting the pink slips and being rather outspoken about it. But they're wrong. Yes, we gave our time. But the soldiers? They gave their lives, their limbs, their futures."

They walked in companionable silence for a bit. Then Mrs. Wilson, the wind out of her sails, spoke more calmly. "Harry doesn't understand. He keeps telling me to relax, to put my feet up – that the war is over and women can go back to their old lives. I've tried. I actually sat in the armchair and put my feet up. I try knitting, I try reading – then I jump up and feel all antsy. I used to enjoy relaxing after coming home from my job – I was exhausted and it felt so good to finally sit down and take a rest." She laughed at the memory. "I remember how much I enjoyed that. Such a little thing."

Lillian wasn't sure how to respond. "It will take some time to readjust."

"The truth is, I don't want to relax. I don't want to be on the sidelines. I want to be out there in the workaday world, in the swirl and rush of workers." She spoke in a tone of fondness. "Mine was not a glamorous job – but it suited me. And I did it well. I know I did. Is it wrong for me to say I was proud of my work? Maybe."

"Of course not. You were recognized for your good work. Promoted. Twice, wasn't it?"

"Yes. Twice, and up for a third. The war years. There was always so much to do, wasn't there? I miss that." She raised her hands, as if in protest. "I'm not saying those were good years. Far from it. Thank God, the war is over! I hope we never have another. So much was – hellish." She shook her head at the thought. "But – I got a little taste of something else. Another way that life could be. That *I* could be. And I miss it." She tightened her headscarf again, simply out of habit. "Ah well. Nothing ever stays the same."

"Have you tried the department stores? They'll be hiring for Christmas."

"I have. In not so many words, they told me the positions have been filled with young gals, and they're sure I would understand." She laughed. "Do I ever! I've been shelved, Mrs. Drooms. That's the long and short of it."

"Oh, don't feel like that. You just have to…" Her words drifted off as they reached Mrs. Wilson's street.

Mrs. Kinney was walking toward them with a bag of groceries and greeted them. "You're not still looking for a job, are you, Mrs. Wilson?" She turned to Lillian. "I keep telling her to enjoy herself. What I wouldn't give for a few days off! Housework is my job and caring for the kids, cooking for the family. What's that quote – 'A man can work from sunup to sundown but a woman's work is never done.' Don't I know it."

They arrived at Mrs. Kinney's stoop and looked up to the second-floor window that was being raised open. Billy's younger brothers stood in the window, hollering down.

"Mom! He called me a nincompoop!"

"That's because he called me a knucklehead!"

Mrs. Kinney rolled her eyes. "See what I mean? Better go. Good seeing you both," she said, and hurried up the steps. She turned back and said to Mrs. Wilson, "And for *my* sake, relax!"

Lillian called up after her. "I think Gabriel is with Billy. I told him to be home in time for dinner, but send him earlier if he's in the way."

"Gabriel? He's never in the way!"

Mrs. Wilson gestured to her brownstone a few doors down. "Well, here's where I turn off. Time to get dinner ready for Harry."

Lillian placed a hand on her shoulder. "Don't be downhearted, Mrs. Wilson. I'm sure things will improve. Somehow."

Never one for pity, the older woman straightened her shoulders. "Oh, don't you worry about me. I'll find some dream to chase. I always do," she said with a laugh, and hurried down the sidewalk.

Lillian watched her leave, and then made her way back home.

*

After leaving the Red String, Billy had taken Gabriel by the arm and hurried him along, not slowing his pace until they reached his street.

"What's up, Billy? Something about business? Money?" Mid-block Gabriel came to a sudden halt, exasperated. "What! Tell me!"

"All right, all right." Billy leaned into Gabriel and spoke in a low voice. "Interested in going into business with me?"

Gabriel gave a shrug. "Sure. I guess so. What do you have in mind?"

Billy led the way to his brownstone and slipped into his movie gangster voice. "I'm talking serious moolah. Big bucks. Lotsa greenbacks."

Gabriel pinned the voice, if not the lines, as James Cagney, Billy's movie hero.

"Why are you being so secretive?"

Billy dropped the accent in surprise. "That's how you're supposed to talk about money and business."

"I already feel guilty," said Gabriel, "and I don't even know what it's about. I don't want to get into trouble. Is it illegal or something?"

"Illegal?" Billy burst into laughter that lasted for some time. "Not at all!"

"Why do you need big bucks, anyway?"

"I told you," Billy said. "For classes. For more movies. For my future career as an actor. And this business is the first step to making it happen."

Instead of going up the brownstone steps, Billy led the way to the basement.

Gabriel looked at him sideways. "So, what kind of business are you talking about?"

"Solid, good old-fashioned business. Just you wait and see." Billy opened the basement door, walked inside and pulled the string to a lightbulb, and waved his arm over to a corner. "There!" Billy crossed his arms and smiled in triumph.

Gabriel scanned the boxes and old shelves and the sheet of beat-up plywood that Billy used to practice his tap dancing on. Next to it stood the only new thing – a red wagon, one wheel askew.

Gabriel looked from the wagon to Billy, and back to the wagon.

"The trans-por-tation business," said Billy, emphasizing each syllable in importance.

"Transportation?"

"And hauling. You and me. Come on. I'll show you." He walked to the wagon and pulled it, but it didn't move because of the broken wheel. "I'll get that fixed. Then – we'll be in business."

Gabriel leaned his head one way, then the other. "This will be our business?"

Billy spread his arms, as if clearing the veils to a vision. "I can see it now. We can carry all sorts of things. Groceries, shopping packages."

Gabriel began to see the possibilities. He walked around the wagon, nodding. "I see what you mean." He smacked Billy on the arm in excitement. "Christmas trees! People always need help carrying those. We can go to that Christmas tree lot."

"Yep," said Billy. "And we'll use our connections for even more business. Mancetti's. Tommy can recommend us to people who don't want to carry their groceries. Mr. G can throw some business our way for larger items. AND – it's the Christmas season! Everyone is shopping and spending money like crazy!"

"I think you're on to something, Billy."

"Righty ho!"

"Hold on. Whose wagon is it?"

"Nobody's. I found it in the park. Abandoned. I guess because of the wheel."

"Are you sure?"

"Sure, I'm sure. Nobody wants a broken wagon. But I can get it fixed. I already talked to Mr. Dunbar at the hardware store. I'll empty by piggy bank and get it fixed."

"Want me to help with the money?"

"Nah. If we decide to paint it, you can buy the paint. Cover up those goofy yellow suns on the sides that some kid probably painted."

Gabriel gave a slow nod. "When would we run this business?"

Billy opened his hands at the possibilities. "After school. Weekends. *While* you're at The Red String."

Gabriel's face lit up. "Makes sense, Billy. Last week I had to help a lady carry an old mantel clock to her home. My arms were burning by the time she opened her door."

"See what I mean?"

"I sure do. How much will we charge?"

"We'll have to think about that. A nickel? A quarter if there's a lot? So much a block? That would add up real fast. That's a lot of matinees, Gabe. You in?"

"Course, I'm in." He reached out his hand for a shake, the only business gesture that came to mind.

Billy first spit on his palm and then gripped Gabriel's hand. "Partners?"

"Partners!" said Gabriel, wiping his hand on his pants.

"Come on. Let's go. In the meantime, let's think of names for our business."

"Sure. I'll come up with some good ones."

Billy turned off the light and closed the basement door. It was already dark outside.

"I better go," said Gabriel. "Let me know when you get the wheel fixed so we can get started."

"I will." He waved at Gabriel as he ran off. "And think of a skit while you're at it!" Billy placed his hands on his hips. "Yep. Things are looking up!"

Chapter 7

Lillian fed Charlotte at the table, or rather, watched Charlotte as she fed herself, getting mashed sweet potatoes and salmon patties all over herself. Lillian wore an unsettled expression, concern filling her eyes.

At the other end of the table, Gabriel worked on his math homework, and Tommy and Charles took notes from the Roman history book for Tommy's report.

Gabriel set aside his homework and began listening to the discussion of Roman heroes and gods, occasionally jotting down information. After a few minutes, he read from his list. "Hercules. Mars. Jupiter."

Charles and Tommy looked over at Gabriel.

"So, Dad," Gabriel asked, "was Hercules stronger than Mars? What about Atlas?"

Charles was momentarily perplexed by Gabriel's sudden participation. "I guess it depends on what type of power you're talking about. Hercules was known for his physical strength and valor, whereas Mars was associated with military prowess. Atlas was technically Greek." He looked at Gabriel to see whether he had answered his question.

Gabriel read over his list. "What sounds better: Hercules Hauling or Mars Moving? Or maybe Jupiter Deliveries?" He tapped his pencil on his cheek.

"Ideas for your school act?" asked Lillian.

"No, a business me and Billy are planning."

"What business is that?" she asked.

"Just carrying packages for people. We're working out the details and I said I'd come up with a name."

Lillian had been thinking all day about Mrs. Wilson, and, even more so, Mrs. Huntington. A sort of pressure was building, a fear that everything was going to fall apart for Mrs. Huntington. After so many years. And Mrs. Wilson. Having worked so hard, so many nights, so many weekends. Always happily, and with pride. Now? *Shelved*, as she had said.

"Gabriel, how did you know that Mrs. Wilson was looking for a job?"

It took him a moment to shift from Roman heroes to Mrs. Wilson. "Oh. I asked her."

"Yes, but *why* did you ask her?"

"I saw her a couple of times in the morning, on my way to school. Dressed up and in a hurry. Like she used to be. I asked her if she was going to a job."

"I see." Lillian sat deep in thought. "Hmm. I think – yes, that's it," she said, musing out loud.

The boys and Charles raised their heads and waited for her to finish.

"What's it, Mom?" asked Tommy.

"Mrs. Wilson, and Mrs. Huntington. They both have a certain air about them." She looked over at Charles. "Almost like an air of loss. Not quite sadness, but something akin to it." She wiped Charlotte's face and fingers. "Mrs. Huntington still has her job, well – a job of sorts. But I think she's hurt that her position went to a new person. The position she created years ago."

Charles, without giving it much thought, said, "Maybe he's the better candidate."

Lillian's head snapped up and she fixed him with a look that demanded an explanation.

"I mean, perhaps your affection for Mrs. Huntington is clouding your judgment."

"That couldn't be further from the truth," Lillian answered sharply. "I've watched her work for a few years now. And though it's only been half a year for Mr. Borland, I can tell you that he's not very capable. He got the position because he's the nephew of one of the directors."

"Was he a soldier?" asked Tommy, trying to find another explanation.

"No, he was not!" Just then Charlotte slammed her hands down on the sweet potato mess, sending splatters onto Lillian's face and blouse. She jumped to her feet and brought the bowl to the sink with a bang. "He did not serve! Flat feet or something."

Charles held his ground. "I don't know either one, so I can't comment on their performance. I'm merely pointing out that the company – looking out for their own interest, mind you – would surely choose the best candidate."

Lillian whipped around as she untied her apron and used it to wipe at her cheek and blouse. "Unlike you, Charles, I have been around several work environments where I've seen this pattern. It's quite clear to a woman. We are judged differently. Our *work* is judged differently. And have you ever heard of someone's *niece* being hired?"

Charles held up his hand defensively. "I can only speak from my experience. I've worked with several women over the years. Mrs. Sullivan being the prime example. And she is given the respect she has earned, regardless of whether she's a woman."

"Are you sure about that?"

Charles had returned his gaze to the book, where Tommy's finger marked a passage. He now looked up, surprised that his judgement was being questioned. "I've worked with her for over twenty-five years."

"I'm merely suggesting that it might be different from her point of view. Have you ever asked her about it?"

"I've never seen the need," Charles snapped. He gave a short laugh, covering the doubt that had suddenly sprouted up inside. "If Mrs. Sullivan had anything to complain about, she would be the first to speak up about it. I see no need to ask her."

"No, you wouldn't."

"What does that mean?"

"Just that things are different for women. They just are. You can't possibly see things from our perspective, can you?" She held up her hand. "And we can't see things from your point of view. But where Mrs. Huntington is concerned, from every angle, she is far superior to Mr. Borland. Her experience, her expertise, her proven record over the years!"

The boys looked from one to the other, surprised by the heat underneath the comments. Gabriel shot a glance to Tommy, who simply focused on his notes.

Lillian began to wash the bowl and spoon in the sink. "There's no point arguing over it. We have two completely different sets of experience." A procession of skirmishes flashed before her from over the years: Mr. Hinkley's relentless antagonism at the department store, Mr. Rockwell's unwanted attentions, and the countless looks and insinuations from men over the years. Then an image came to her mind, unbidden, of her mother – washing dishes at the kitchen sink, looking out the window with an air of wistfulness. Lillian felt her eyes tingle with mounting tears.

She swallowed her feelings, dried her hands and dabbed at her eyes. Then she lifted Charlotte and carried her to the bedroom.

Charles watched her leave, surprised at her reaction. "Why don't you finish this page, Tommy. Let's go over your math problems, Gabriel. It's getting late."

Charles continued to help the boys with their homework for another hour. He then glanced through a file from work while Lillian gave Charlotte a bath and put her to bed. He was nagged by a feeling of guilt – alongside a sense of being in the right – and stubbornly nursed both. But that ugly jaggedness only made him feel worse. Why was she so upset?

After the boys went to bed, Charles sat on the couch and tried to read the history book. Why hadn't he simply listened to her? Why had he gotten so defensive? He had seen the moment when she hung her head at the sink and it hurt him. He no longer cared about who was right or wrong. It wasn't like them to argue like this.

When Lillian came into the living room, he set down his book and gave her a tender smile.

Lillian had also softened by then. Charlotte was asleep, and the boys were talking in their bedroom. She was also wondering why they had argued, why she had snapped at Charles. They were bound to disagree on things. Tired from the day, she put on a smile and sat down next to him.

He reached out and took her hand. "Charlotte's asleep?"

"Yes. Finally. Five lullabies later." She let out a deep breath.

An unspoken truce fell quietly around them.

"Tommy seems happy with his project. You're a good teacher, Charles."

He shrugged the comment away. "It's a subject that interests me. He's a quick learner. He asks interesting questions. I think his paper will be strong."

Lillian smiled. "Good."

"Lillian," Charles began. "I didn't mean to say anything hurtful. I know how much you admire and like Mrs. Huntington. And I don't know her. The few times I've met her with you, she struck me as a very fine person. I'm sure she's extremely capable."

"It's not that, Charles."

He waited for her to say more. When she remained silent, he tried to explain himself, feeling that he had been misunderstood and misjudged. "You know that I was raised by a strong mother, who was my father's equal on the farm, and ran it after his death. And my sister Kate. You see what she is. And her daughters." He was beginning to feel more secure in his position. "And your sister. Annette seems to have as much say in the running of the orchard as Bernie does."

Lillian had to smile. "If not more."

"We've both had strong women in our lives."

Lillian lightly pressed her fingers to the bridge of her nose. "I'm sorry I snapped at you. I was speaking about something general, larger – not you and your comments." She tried to retrace her earlier thoughts. "It was Gabriel's comment, I suppose. I've been thinking about Mrs. Wilson lately. That look of loss, or longing – for something that was only barely there. Getting a taste, a tantalizing glimpse of something – and then having it taken away."

He waited for her to continue, doing his utmost to follow. "I guess I don't know what you mean."

They sat in silence for a few moments, each pursuing their own thoughts. Then Lillian spoke softly, remembering the first time she had these feelings. Feelings that had lain dormant for long years, never really finding expression. "I was a teenager when I first visited the Metropolitan Museum. With my parents and Annette."

Charles wondered at this topic. It seemed unrelated to Mrs. Wilson and Mrs. Huntington. He gave a sound, hoping it showed his interest.

"We took the train early, packed a lunch, and spent all day at the museum. It was wonderful. It really opened my world, the wealth of human expression, the craftsmanship, the artistry, the beauty."

Lillian's face shifted from an expression of awe to a more tender memory. "I saw how happy Mom was. She knew how much I would love it, and it gave her such joy to see my happiness. We saw as much as we could, and it so fueled my appetite for more. I think that was when I really took becoming an artist seriously."

Charles made a few more sounds of understanding and stroked her hair as she spoke.

"But on our way back, on the train – it was evening by then – I realized that something was bothering me. Dad and Annette had dozed off. Mom smiled across at me and raised her eyebrows. She could always read me so well. 'What is it?' she asked.

"It took me a while to find the words. 'Everything – almost everything – in that huge museum – treasures from hundreds, even thousands, of years ago – was made by men, wasn't it?'

"Mom simply nodded, but there was a different look in her eyes. 'Does it make you wonder what women would have created?'

"'Yes. It does.' She took my hand and held it for a few moments. Then we both looked out the window.

"I remember realizing that the world I lived in was in essence a male world. And it filled me with a sense of loss, for something that was forever gone. I wondered how much wasn't created, wasn't expressed – or simply, wasn't valued. How much of history we never heard about. Where were the women? What were they doing? What were they thinking? What did they value? Yes, there are novels by women. But even those are relatively recent, and describe the world they were allowed access to. Maybe it's just an obvious fact I'm stating. But that museum trip made it clear to me."

Charles recalled a trip to the Met with Lillian and the boys and tried to remember what he had seen. The armor room fascinated the boys, of course. The medieval rooms. He remembered the statues and paintings – women were certainly represented. Mostly young, lovely women. Wives of famous men. Historical subjects, Greek and Roman statues of goddesses, eternally youthful and beautiful. But wasn't that simply a celebration of female beauty? An homage to women? Or, was that what the emperors and kings and patrons wanted to see hanging in their surroundings? If he was such a patron, he would surely prefer the same.

Then his memory took him to the busts of Caesars and Roman senators, many of them older, mature men. Paintings of heroic warriors, the epic battles. The Renaissance merchants and burghers, also older. But he couldn't recall any works that were painted or sculpted *by* women. What would they have created? He briefly imagined the entire history of women as taking place in a sort of timeless, universal kitchen. There they labored, oblivious to the world outside, busily cooking and cleaning and taking care of others...

Lillian shifted, and searched for words. "I think – I think that feeling I had back then is what I see in the faces of Mrs. Wilson and Mrs. Huntington. Not just anger or resentment – but a feeling of loss. A loss that creates a yearning." She turned her questioning face to Charles. "A shapeless yearning that's difficult to grapple with." She shook her head in disappointment, aware that she wasn't finding the right words. Or that perhaps the feeling was outside of words.

"I'm glad you told me. It – it makes me see things a little differently. I think."

They sat quietly, physically close, and tender towards each other – but with something between them. As if they stood inches away from each other, but on two separate landmasses.

"I know these things have been on your mind, lately." Charles turned towards her. "Lillian, I don't want you to think I take you for granted. But I can't help comparing my life *with* you to the way it was *before* you. All those years of coming home tired from work to a dark apartment. Opening a can of soup for dinner. Then working on papers into the night." He grimaced at the emptiness of his old life. "What I have with you is a real home. Full of life and love and happiness. And I'm so grateful. It's the high point of my day, walking through that door."

"I understand, Charles. And that makes me happy. I had that too growing up. Mom was always home. But there were times I wondered if she longed for more – wanted a larger world, a greater role."

Charles waited to hear more. He began to wonder if the same had been true for his mother. "Like what? I mean, what made you think that?"

"Oh, little things. Sometimes I would come home from school and find her seated at the piano, picking out melodies on the keys. I would silently watch her from the next room, and slowly fill with a sad sense of regret for her. She never learned to play. I wish… I wish she could have. I think she would have loved it." Lillian squinted into the past. "I felt like she was getting a tiny glimmer of something when she touched the keys. A way that things could be. That *she* could be. A different way of connecting with the world. I wished she could have had more opportunities. But she never complained."

Charles had never questioned whether his mother might have wanted more. Had he missed seeing this silent longing? Now that he thought of it, he was sure that she must have yearned for more. The farm was hard. Her life was hard. He looked to Lillian, as if to make sure he wasn't missing anything a second time.

"Did you play the piano?" asked Charles.

"Yes. Mom made sure of that. Annette and I loved playing. One of the many gifts she gave us."

Charles grew mildly troubled. "I never knew that about you." He wondered what else he didn't know about her. Were there other things that were important to her that he was ignorant of? Was he not curious enough about her? About her life before him?

He reached out and took her hand. "Did you have a piano after you left home? After you were married?"

"Oh, no. There was no money – or time – for that, once we moved to the city."

A small cry from Charlotte caused Lillian to jump to her feet and check on her, putting the conversation to an end. When she came back, she tidied up the kitchen, and then got ready for bed.

Charles read a few more pages in the Roman history book, or tried to. The stories suddenly didn't seem very relevant to him. He flashed on the myth of Romulus, his treachery against the

Sabines, various stories of greed and betrayal, the countless wars… The world's history in miniature? He rubbed his eyes, and closed the book. Then he turned off the lights, and went to bed.

Lillian was almost asleep when she heard Charles say, "Would you like to have a piano, Lillian?"

She laughed and snuggled into him. "Are you still thinking about that? No, Charles."

"We could put one in the alcove, near the window. You could play it whenever you felt like it."

"Where my drawing table is? No. I need every inch of my studio. I need a larger table as it is." She gave a yawn and added, "Maybe some-day…"

Then almost on the verge of sleep again, she added playfully, "But I wouldn't mind a phono-graph."

They fell asleep entwined, their under-standing of each other deepened by the weaving together of the foreign lands of separate youths.

Chapter 8

Charles and Mason walked back to the office together after an outside meeting, enjoying the festive atmosphere of the avenues, and talking about plans for the holiday.

"It adds something special to have Alice back home for Christmas," said Mason. "It's like old times. Three of the four sisters, together again. Though I was hoping Edith could have been here."

"Twice in one year might have been too much for them to manage," said Charles.

"True. A whole month over the summer with her and Desmond – what more could I ask for?"

Charles looked at him askance. "I know the answer to that."

Mason smiled. "I admit, I was hoping that being in New York City again would make them want to move back. But they're happy with California and their jobs. At least for now. I'm quite proud of them both."

"Even without Edith here, you'll have a full house."

"Packed to the rim. The kids running around, my sisters coming and going. That's the way our Christmases have always been." Mason grew momentarily serious. "I do worry about Claudia. I wish she'd get on with her life. She's the only one not married. What is she waiting for?"

Charles had to laugh. "Sounds like a reversal of a few years ago, when you *didn't* want Edith to marry."

"The bossy older brother," Mason said with a chuckle. "That's what Susan says, too."

After a moment he added, "I thought I had learned my lesson. I vowed to stay out of the love lives of my sisters. But I do think she's making a mistake. She's finishing her degree on electrical engineering, of all things. It made sense during the war, when she worked with the WAVES. Working with radio transmissions, and reports on decoded messages, and – all that". The wave of his hand indicated that he had very little understanding of what Claudia had actually worked on.

"I'd think you would be proud of her. It sounds like a tremendous accomplishment for a woman."

"Yes, it is. But then what? There will be no jobs open to her. I've tried to tell her it will be an uphill battle at best. That she's just setting herself up for failure. I'd rather see her happily married, kids all around her." His eyes filled with concern. "She's different from the younger two. More serious. As a WAVE she lived in the barracks – one of those converted hotels, you know – and took her job very seriously. I think that experience changed her. Matured her. It definitely made her much more independent. She knows what she wants and is going after it."

"Well, you never know…"

Mason stared at the sidewalk as they continued their way back to the office. "Thank goodness her coursework included clerical training. I suppose she can always work as a secretary somewhere. At one of those radio and communications companies. RCA, AT&T. Maybe Western Union." Mason tugged at his ear. "Those are places she's mentioned. I guess she knows what she's talking about."

"Other than Edith, I don't really know your sisters. But Edith always spoke very highly of them. Especially Claudia."

Mason bristled a bit at that comment. "I think Edith has influenced her. Over the summer, they had long conversations about her future. They write to each other regularly. Edith wants her to take the train and visit them out in California next year. I don't want Claudia moving out there, too."

"It's certainly worked for Edith. She's both happily married and working. Edith is very level-headed. I will always be grateful for her help in the office, during those years we were so short staffed."

Mason glanced over at Charles with a faint smile of pride. "Yes, that worked out well, didn't it?"

"Tremendously well." They waited at the corner for the light to change, then crossed the street. Charles's thoughts turned to the recent conversations with Lillian.

"I don't think that would be possible now, would it?" he added.

"You mean…"

"The way we were encouraged to turn to women for the workforce. We had no choice."

"No, it's all different now. More like it used to be." Mason's mouth gave the equivalent of a shrug. "And everyone seems happy about it. For the most part."

"I have to admit I was happy with their work. The women," said Charles. "Sorry to see them go. But it was their choice, and I'm happy for them. Can't expect them to be cooped up in factories and offices all their lives. Most of them are married now, and starting families."

"In a way that we were *not* sorry to see Willard Hall go. He was a troublemaker. Glad he left of his own accord. Wish he would have taken Eric and Bo with him. I just don't care for those two."

"No?" Charles had to consider Mason's comment. Over the years, he had come to trust Mason's judgement implicitly. "Eric's a competent accountant. I can't find anything to fault him with."

"There's something about him that rubs me the wrong way. He complains to anyone who will listen that Mrs. Sullivan oversteps her authority with him. I've overheard him a few times, putting her down in front of the others. Ostensibly in a playful manner, but it's unkind, the things he says."

"Really?" asked Charles, surprised. "I haven't noticed anything."

"He's careful to toe the line when you're there. He says demeaning things about her being a woman, or alludes to her age."

Charles discounted the complaint. "Surely, it's in jest. She hasn't said anything about it." He remembered Lillian's words again, and had a moment of doubt. "Do you think I should speak to her about it?"

"She can take care of herself. No need to get involved in that sort of thing." Mason looked into a restaurant that had Christmas lights around the door. "Did Lillian tell you about the Christmas lunch the girls are planning."

"The girls?"

"Mrs. Sullivan, Lillian, and her friend Izzy. And, they've invited Claudia. Most likely at Edith's suggestion. Mrs. Sullivan would still do anything for Edith. They were quite a team."

"Ah, yes. Lillian mentioned how much she was looking forward to it. A holiday lunch. She doesn't get out as much as she used to." He thought again about Lillian and her different perspective on things. "Mason, do you think the office feels – balanced – with so many of the women gone?"

"Don't talk to me about balance! I've been completely outnumbered by women all my life! My mother, four sisters, three daughters. Thank goodness I have one son. We're planning an outing while they do their Christmas activities – shopping, baking, and whatnot," he said in a dismissive tone. "We're going bowling!" Mason gave a playful smack to Charles's arm. "Why don't you and your boys come along? We'll have our own Christmas outing."

"Bowling!" Charles smiled at the idea. "I used to enjoy that. I think the boys would like it."

They entered the office building and climbed the stairs to the floor of Drooms & Mason Accounting and went on to discuss their sons, and their school projects and jobs.

"Gabriel's been talking about another job that he and his friend Billy are doing. Carrying Christmas trees, that kind of thing."

"Work is good for boys. Helps prepare them for their futures."

Charles nodded. "He's quite fired up about it. I'll speak to them about bowling. Give them something new to look forward to."

As they neared the office, the door flew open and Miss Wynn came out, brushing away the tears on her cheeks, and went the other direction towards the Ladies Room.

"Hmm," said Charles. "I wonder what prompted that?"

"Some heartache with a beau, no doubt. Still, we don't need that kind of thing in the office. It isn't professional."

"I'll have Mrs. Sullivan speak to her about it. Oh, and I'll have her start on the annual Christmas party."

"Always a cheerful way to end the year. And what a good year it has been!" Mason said with a smile, and with that the two men entered the office.

*

"Holy mackerel!" Billy counted the latest tip and added it up in his head. "That makes one dollar and fifty-five cents – and it's only our first week!" cried Billy. "That pays for repairing the wheel with plenty left over for us. Now I can finish paying off Mr. G for the tap shoes he found for me."

"Mr. G can find anything," Gabriel said with pride.

"He pretty much gave them to me for free, with your discount. Where else can you find tap shoes for under a dollar? Barely used!"

"He said to make sure you bring the wagon by on Saturday. That the Christmas shoppers might need help."

"Swell!" said Billy. "Come on. Let's go back to Mancetti's. We have about a half hour before we have to go home. Who knows, we could make another quarter!"

After twenty minutes, it became clear that no one wanted help with deliveries. Everyone could carry a bag of groceries by themselves. Billy and Gabriel sat outside Mancetti's in the wagon, legs draped over the side, not bothered by the lull.

"I'll ask Tommy when the big shoppers come in," said Gabriel. "I know Mrs. Sanders comes on Wednesdays and always asks Tommy to help her carry her bags home."

"And we need to go to the Christmas tree lot more often. People are really starting to buy their trees and wreaths and stuff." Billy smiled at the acting classes he would be able to take, lining them up in his mind. "I can take a lot of classes. And the matinees!" He gently elbowed Gabriel. "Speaking of acting, we have to hand in our idea. I haven't thought of anything. Have you?"

Gabriel rubbed his chin. "Ten minutes isn't long. So, we won't have to spend a lot of time rehearsing and memorizing. And they said we'll get the last act as long as it's patriotic. And entertaining enough."

"I can make sure of that. What do you think, Gabe?"

"Well, we could write a short scene, say, about George Washington. We could make up how he spent Christmas – carving toys for kids or something. Or – how about this? The Queen Mary carrying men back after the war?"

"Sounds too complicated. Let's keep it simple, Gabe."

"How about you recite something –"

"Like the Gettysburg Address? No, thank you!"

"We have to think of something, Billy! *You* come up with an idea. It's your show."

"Don't ask me. I'm just a song and dance man."

Gabriel rolled his eyes at Billy's oft-quoted line from a James Cagney movie.

Then Billy shot out of the wagon. "That's it!"

Gabriel looked around. "What's it?"

"Jimmy Cagney!"

"What about him"?

"Not just any James Cagney." Billy transformed his posture and face into his idol. "Who am I?" He then broke out into a remarkable forward-leaning brisk walk, bent at the waist, legs stiff, arms swinging at his side.

Then Gabriel also jumped out of the wagon. "George M. Cohan! In *Yankee Doodle Dandy*! Why didn't we think of it sooner?"

Billy checked off the requirements on his fingers. "It's short. It's patriotic. And I'll make sure it's *plenty* entertaining. Come on! Business can wait. Let's go do a quick tryout in the basement."

They ran, pulling the wagon behind him, all the way to Billy's brownstone.

"Do you know all the words?" asked Gabriel

"Do I know all the words!" Billy repeated in exaggeration. "You bet." Then he stopped to thump himself on the chest, in character. "And that ain't no josh. I'm a Yankee, by gosh!" – a line from the movie he liked to annoy Mickey with.

"How many times have you seen the movie, Billy?"

"Seven? Eight? I think I know all the words and can hum the ones I forget."

"Mrs. Taggert down the hall has a Victrola and she has the record," said Gabriel. "She's nice. She'll let us listen to it whenever we want."

"Swell! You might have to do some of the chorus singing. But don't worry. We'll cut out anything boring."

*

After their quick rehearsal, Gabriel was pumped up with energy and decided his news would cheer up his friend Hap. He eyed the sky and decided he had just enough time to run into the park and see if Hap was there.

He wasn't in the usual places and Gabriel almost gave up, assuming he must have gone home, or found a day job. But as he was leaving, he saw a man huddled on a bench. He stopped and peered closer. It was Hap all right, but he looked different. His army overcoat hung extra loose on him and his hair looked like it hadn't been combed for a long time. And he hadn't shaved around his beard. He looked like a worn-out hobo.

Gabriel walked up to him gently. "Hey, Hap. How you doing?"

Hap had been staring at the ground. He raised his head and blinked at Gabriel, slowly coming back to the present. "Oh. Gabriel."

Gabriel sat next to him. "Everything okay?"

Hap gave a shrug. "It's not one way or another. It just is."

"What do you mean, Hap?"

He stared off, glassy eyed. "It's like I'm wandering around No Man's Land, seeing all the mud and barbed wire and dead soldiers and body parts – just walking around it all, like it's my home, or final resting place. The end for me." He looked at Gabriel and gave a rough laugh. "But the funny thing is, there's no one on either side – no armies. Both sides have gone home. No good guys, no bad guys. Just me."

Gabriel rubbed Hap's shoulder. "Maybe sitting out here all alone isn't a good idea, Hap. Maybe it makes you think too much about the war."

Hap nodded. "Yeah. I'll be going home. They'll be serving dinner soon." He rubbed at his eyes. "Sorry, Gabriel. I didn't mean to pull you down. You look happy about something."

"I am. Thought I'd come and tell you about it. My friend and I found a way to make some money. Thought you might like to help us. Hauling, transporting stuff."

Hap appeared pained by the kindness. "Thanks, Gabriel. But I'm – I'm not up to it. I don't think I'd be good for business."

Gabriel rubbed Hap's shoulder again, thinking that he seemed even thinner. "Maybe later. When you're feeling better." Gabriel looked around the park. It was starting to grow dimmer. He knew he had to leave soon, but he didn't want to leave his friend feeling so sad. He had to find a way to get him out of No Man's Land. "Hey!" he said brightly. "We figured out our skit for school. Did you ever see the movie *Yankee Doodle Dandy*?"

"Sure, I did. Guess we all did. The glorification of the Great War." He gave a mirthless laugh.

"We only have ten minutes, so Billy's going to sing that song. And dance. He can make anything look good. He loves that movie."

Hap gave another chuckle. "*Yankee Doodle Dandy*. At the end, what happens? You remember?"

Gabriel smiled at the image that came to mind. "I sure do. He's an old man by then. And he tap dances down the stairs."

"After that."

Gabriel looked up at the sky, to the left, then to the right. "I forget. What happens?"

"He joins a parade of soldiers. Going to war. Another war." He muttered, as if to himself, "Rounding up the cannon fodder." He gave a low groan. "All those songs and movies are about the beginning. Healthy men in one piece, smiling, happy. Or maybe later when they're fighting and winning. None of those movies show them coming back home. If they come back at all. Because if they showed guys like us, like me, no one would go to the next war."

Gabriel tipped his head, considering the words. "Maybe that would be good. As long as the other side did the same thing."

"A simple solution!" Hap leaned back and gave a genuine laugh. "You're a good kid, Gabriel."

They sat in silence for a few moments. Then Hap grew serious again, and peered into the distance. "If ever I'm not here, Gabriel, don't worry. Okay?"

"Okay. Where will you be?"

Hap squinted into the distance. "Visiting my buddies. Thinking it's about time."

"Your war buddies?"

"That's right."

Gabriel smiled. "I bet they'll be real happy to see you." He gave another glance at the sky and got to his feet. "I better go. Mom gets worried when it starts to get dark."

"I remember your ma. A lovely lady. You're a lucky kid."

Then Hap stood and held out his hand. "Goodbye, Gabriel."

Chapter 9

Lillian left the apartment with a small portfolio tucked under her arm. It held her latest children's drawings and she was looking forward to showing them to Mrs. Huntington. At least she hoped that Mrs. Huntington would be the one to review her work. This was a project they had been working on for quite some time, both of them excited about the third book in a series by a well-establish children's author. Lillian also wanted to discuss some ideas about the women and work series.

She decided to walk down to her old street and cut through the park to the East Side, and then catch a downtown bus. Up ahead she saw Mrs. Wilson, looking very much as she used to – brisk, fired up, her enthusiasm topped with a wide smile.

"Lillian!" Mrs. Wilson hollered, and hurried to catch up with her. "Where are you off to? Your wonderful job, by the looks of it."

"Good afternoon, Mrs. Wilson! Yes. I have some sketches to drop off to Mrs. Huntington.

How are you? I must say, you look quite transformed from the last time I saw you. Did you find – are you –"

"A job? Not exactly. But my search is over! I have found a worthy purpose. I don't know why I didn't think of it earlier."

"What wonderful news! I can see how happy it has made you. What is it?"

Mrs. Wilson beamed, let a few moments of joy build, and then said brightly: "The Maharajah!"

Lillian's smile froze as she tried to make sense of the response. She must have misunderstood her. "The Mah–"

"Yes, the Good Maharajah, as he's called. Oh, I'm sure you remember reading about him. The Indian prince who took in all those children who surely would have died if not for his actions."

Lillian looked away as she recalled the story. "Refugee children. I do remember reading about that. In '42, wasn't it?"

"Polish children. They called him *Bapu* – father. Now that the war is over, many of them are being returned to parents or relatives that have been found."

"What an extraordinary story. I remember how, at the time, it gave me such hope in humanity." Lillian now looked at Mrs. Wilson. "But how does that…"

"There are millions of orphans all over Europe. Millions! Starving, struggling to survive. Shouldn't we all do what we can for them? Drives for clothing and money are all well and good, but they can't compare to a loving home, can they?"

"You mean – you want to adopt orphans?"

"I have an empty bedroom. I have time. Goodness, shouldn't I try to help at least one of those children?"

Lillian tried to take it all in. It seemed an astonishing thing to undertake – and yet, it was clearly the right thing to do. But Mrs. Wilson was surely in her mid-fifties. In ten years –

"I know what you're thinking. I'm too old. But I have the same energy I had twenty years ago."

Lillian blushed on realizing that Mrs. Wilson had so accurately read her mind. "I was just thinking that perhaps an older child would be more feasible. For you, and Harry."

"I know. Harry says I'm being idealistic and that I miss the old days when our kids were young. Our two boys are grown men, married now. Both living upstate. But it's not that. It's about carrying on as I did during the war years. Doing what was necessary. Doing my best. And what's better than helping a child? To make them happy, to help them believe in goodness." She gestured to Lillian, as if proving her point. "The laughter of Charlotte, the high jinks of Gabriel and Billy, the earnestness of Tommy. Isn't that where happiness and hope lie?"

Lillian's face softened. "Absolutely. You are absolutely right." She gave it some thought, then nodded in agreement. "It's a lot to take on, a lot of time and energy. But if anyone can do it, it's you."

Now that Lillian seemed to understand, Mrs. Wilson's eyes lit up again. "I'll take any child that they can give me. But I would dearly love a little girl. I can almost see her standing there, looking hopeful, with two long braids. I haven't looked into it yet, all the details, and I need to convince Harry. But it feels right."

"I admire your decision. Do let me know what you find out."

Mrs. Wilson squeezed her arm. "I will. I hope I can make it happen soon. But you're in a hurry." She started to leave then turned around. "I'm off to buy some holly and pine boughs. I am now officially in the Christmas spirit! Ta-ta!"

That was indeed the old Mrs. Wilson, Lillian thought. Cheerful, determined, filled with purpose.

As Lillian hurried to meet with Mrs. Huntington, her mind filled with a jumble of images, the way it did when she first conceived of a book cover. She imagined a group of thin and weary Polish children, Indian summer palaces and palm trees, clinking bangles and fluttering saris. And a radiant Mrs. Wilson holding out her arms to a lost little girl with two long braids.

She carried the enthusiasm with her to her meeting with Mrs. Huntington. Her sketches were praised, but they would have to be approved by Mr. Borland's office. And any discussion about the women and work series would also have to be continued with him.

"Of course," Lillian responded with a professional smile. But she couldn't hide her disappointment. This was a new way of working.

Mrs. Huntington walked with Lillian down the corridor. "I'm sure Mr. Borland will be pleased with your work. I don't think you have to worry about that." She glanced around her, and spoke softly. "Just between us, Lillian, I might be leaving soon. I'd like to talk to you about it."

A demanding voice came from her old office. "Mrs. Huntington!"

She pressed Lillian's arm. "I'll call you."

For the second time that afternoon, Lillian was speechless. She walked down the corridor and pressed the elevator button, her mind scattering in several directions. She had never considered the possibility that Mrs. Huntington would not be there.

Her walk home was distinctly different from her walk to the meeting. She felt deflated, sad, confused, her energy drained.

When she reached home, she was greeted by Charles who had just arrived a few minutes ahead of her. He sat at one end of the couch, his briefcase on his lap, and sifted through some work papers.

Tommy, seated in the armchair near the couch, gave her an update on Charlotte, who was now sound asleep. "And I'm working on my Christmas list," he said. "Dad's helping me."

"I need to get started on mine," she said, kissing the top of his head. She hung her coat in the hall closet and set her portfolio in her alcove studio.

She saw that Gabriel was staring out the window to where he could see the tree tops of Central Park. His stillness let her know that he was pondering something.

"Hi, Mom."

"What are you so deep in thought about, Gabriel?" she asked.

"Just thinking about Hap."

"Oh. Mr. Coleman." She sat down on the couch next to Charles and leaned into him. Gabriel walked over and sat across from them.

"You know," Lillian said to Gabriel, "I suddenly remembered why his name rang a bell. It came up a few weeks ago, at the hospital. I was just finishing up with my class, when the coordinator mentioned it. Apparently, his brother has been looking for him. The last address he had for Hap was the hospital, then he seemed to disappear."

"He doesn't like to be around a lot of people. But wouldn't he want to see his family?"

"You'd think so." Lillian rested her head on the back of the couch.

"Do you think there's anything we can do for him?" asked Gabriel. "Tell his family where he is?"

"That would break patient confidentiality. We have to respect his choices."

Gabriel looked down at the floor, twisting his hands. "I think – he seemed different yesterday. I keep thinking about him."

"Different how?" asked Charles.

"Like he was extra sad. He said he might go see his buddies. I thought that would be a good thing. When I left, he shook my hand. He always says 'see you later,' but this time he said 'goodbye.' Like he's going to be gone for a while."

Lillian exchanged a look with Charles.

Gabriel waited to see how she would respond.

"It's hard to say," Lillian said. "I'll be at the hospital for class tomorrow. Maybe I can try to speak to someone about his condition. Find out when he was last seen by a doctor."

"He doesn't go there anymore," said Gabriel. "He told me they treated his leg and it's fine now, but they can't fix his nerves. Something like that. Then he went to have dinner, at the boarding house."

Tommy called Gabriel over to him and they were soon discussing ideas for presents to give. He whispered something that caused Gabriel's eyes to light up.

Lillian looked off, trying to better remember Mr. Coleman when he was a patient at the hospital. "For the most part, he seemed like a kind, gentle man. Helpful with the other patients."

Charles set his work papers down. "Those other kinds of wounds can be difficult to treat. I remember from the last war, how many of us struggled for years. Some, for the rest of their lives. He'll have to find something that gives him meaning. Family. Work. Something that keeps the darkness at bay."

Lillian rubbed her neck and thought of Izzy. "Like Red. Izzy said he often struggles with the effects of all those years."

Charles nodded. "He was in it for a long time. I can see the signs in him, the quiet struggle. But I think he'll get through it all right. It helps that he has someone like Izzy."

That comment brought a smile to Lillian's tired face. "She has enough fight in her for two."

She told Charles about the meeting and Mrs. Huntington's words about leaving. He tried to comfort her by saying that it might or might not happen and to wait and see, not to worry about it for now. She agreed and enjoyed a few more moments of his nearness. Then she sat up. "I guess it's time to get dinner started."

*

Izzy and Red ordered another round of drinks after their meal at an uptown pub. They both had their chins in their hands, downcast. Izzy had failed to lighten Red's mood after he had yet another disagreement at the family business, this time over Red's friend, Joe Sanchez. This argument was more like a fallout, with his father, uncle, and cousins on one side, and Red all alone on the other.

"So, they don't want Sanchez. And he's moving back to Texas," Izzy repeated.

Red took a swig of beer and nodded. "His family is there..." His voice trailed off, then he sat up in anger. "We served together! Bled together, cried together, got drunk together, risked our lives for each other! Then we come back – and we can't WORK together? What the hell's wrong with everyone! It makes no sense." He put his head in his hands.

"Oh, Red," Izzy sighed. "A lot of things don't make sense. It's messy human nature we're always up against." She had run out of arguments and other points of view. Then she decided on the obvious one. "Be honest – are you happy working for your family?"

That took the fire out of Red and he leaned back and looked saddened. "I really wanted to be. I tried to be. It's what I thought about for years over there. But I just don't fit."

Izzy leaned forward and took his hands. "Did you ever? It's okay to be different from them, Red. You can still love them. Maybe even better with some distance between you."

"Dad – he's never been the same since Mom died. Seems lost. Just goes along with his older brother." He put his hands around his glass and stared into it. "God, I miss her. That was one of the worst things about the war – the years I lost being with Mom, enjoying her company. When I came back, I was different, Mom was sick…" He took a slower sip and looked out at nothing.

Izzy didn't want him to go down that road. She squeezed his hands and gave them a light shake. "Listen, Red. This could be a good thing. We're doing all right with money. I'm happy working at Rockwell. I'll be there another ten years! Once you're finished with your degree, you can work anywhere. Start looking around, see what's out there. We'll still get a house – but it doesn't have to be right away. Maybe it's best to wait and see what's up ahead. I'm game. This will be good for us, Red. We'll strike out on our own!"

For the first time, Red smiled and his eyes came to life. He looked at Izzy with love. "I think you're right, Iz. I haven't been happy. I don't know what I want. But no, I'm not happy there." He brought her hands to his lips and kissed them. "So, we'll strike out on our own. I like the sound of that."

With a sense of relief, they left their drinks, paid the bill, and cut through Central Park, making plans for their new future.

Chapter 10

After her holiday lunch with Mrs. Sullivan, Izzy, and Claudia, Lillian caught the uptown bus. It had been good to get out and visit with them. Except for when her sister, Annette, was visiting the city, or the occasional lunch with Izzy, she rarely went out.

But today the bus was crowded, the horns and traffic jarring – she felt the need for air, space. She glanced at her watch – she had a good hour before she had to pick up Charlotte and get started on dinner.

Even though it was lightly snowing, she made a quick decision to get off on 57th Street and cut through Central Park. An undercurrent of tension propelled her choice. She knew it had to do with the unsettling situation with Mrs. Huntington, her mentor and champion. And friend. Over the past two years, they had increasingly confided in each other and truly enjoyed one another's company.

As she made her way to the park, she realized that her discontent also came, surprisingly, from today's luncheon. But why? It had been so wonderful to see everyone. They all had good news to share, and everyone was looking forward to the Christmas season. What was prodding her, pulling her down?

It had started off so well. Lillian had decided to wear her new cobalt blue dress, with the pearls from Charles. She had only worn it once since she bought it and was happy to have another occasion to enjoy it.

Izzy, always so smart and fashionable, dazzled in a stunning purple suit dress. Without even trying, Izzy lived in the spotlight, seemingly indifferent to the eyes that always landed on her. Her style merged with her confident personality and always drew stares.

Lillian was touched to see that Mrs. Sullivan wore a dress, deep green with a subtle pattern, and her Christmas brooch at the neckline. Lillian had rarely seen her wear anything but her sensible tweed suits. She realized that Mrs. Sullivan's life with Brendan had allowed for a touch more glamour. Lillian wondered if the older woman had longed for it all those years before him.

Claudia had worn a simple gray skirt and blouse set that Lillian recognized as Edith's. As Claudia later explained over lunch, for the past two years she had practically lived in her WAVES suits and didn't need much else. However, the scarlet scarf she wore around her neck set off her simple, understated beauty, and offered a shimmer of holiday color.

There had been much laughter – Izzy's effervescence and Mrs. Sullivan's wit made sure of that. Claudia had been somewhat reserved, never having lunched with any of them before, except once over the summer with Edith at her side. Lillian noticed that Claudia was a keen listener and had questions about how they were handling their work, the changes, their futures.

They all seemed to be struggling with their jobs in one way or another.

Mrs. Sullivan was the first to speak up. "I have the best of both worlds. I'm delighted to be back in the office." She tasted her soup, and after some thought added, "It's different, of course. That's to be expected. I sometimes don't feel welcome there, a surprise after so many years. There's a recently rehired fellow, who worked there before the war, stirring up trouble. He taunts the younger gals, tells them it's time to go home and have babies. Take care of their men. Last week he belittled their work, saying that a monkey could file and what was taking them so long. At which point I set a stack of papers in front of him and told him in that case, he could do his own filing. He retaliated by picking on Darla, one of the shy girls. She burst into tears and had to take refuge in the powder room, until she could compose herself." Then, as if realizing that she was perhaps saying too much, she gave a hearty laugh. "It's on such days that I wish Edith was still here!"

Lillian had listened, growing increasingly concerned. "Does Charles know about this behavior?"

"Oh, in a general way. I don't mean to speak against the office. And I certainly don't want to add to his load. For the most part, we all get along and pull our own weight. And I'm a firm believer that work is good for one. To be kept busy, and engaged, and to be physically tired at the end of the day. That's all good. The other unpleasant parts, well, that's just part of life, isn't it?"

Izzy agreed with her. "And if the war years have taught us anything, it's how to solve our own problems, and not go running to someone else."

Perhaps that was it, Lillian now thought. Though they had talked at their luncheon about the new fashions, the abundance of goods, and the booming economy, the conversation had a way of turning to women and their lives, before, during, and now, after the war.

Izzy was secure and happy in her job, but she gave examples of friends and relatives, women who had done so much during the war, and then had gone back home to take care of others or to get married – after doing the most admirable, and even heroic, jobs. Such as a cousin who was one of the "Donut Dollies," the morale-boosting Red Cross volunteers who drove and handed out donuts and coffee on the front lines in Europe. How some of them had even found themselves in foxholes! Risking their lives for the soldiers.

Claudia pointed out the millions of women who had worked in defense plants. She had several stories about women who worked in a munitions factory, working long shifts handling explosive materials – and some of the accidents, and even deaths, that occurred.

Only at Izzy's prompting did Claudia talk about her time in the WAVES, working with radio transmissions and intercepts, and preparing reports for the officers. She tended to minimize the importance of her role, compared to the work of others. And she made sure to point out that, "For the last several months, as men began to return, my duties had shifted to clerical work." She gave a bright smile. "All in all, it was a remarkable experience and I'm so grateful I had the opportunity."

Lillian thought it sounded quite extraordinary, but Claudia made light of it and said she had just been doing her part, like everyone else.

"Goodness!" Lillian exclaimed. "And on top of that, Charles said that you're finishing a college degree. In something with radios?"

Claudia nodded. "I just completed my degree. I took college courses at night studying electrical engineering, especially in radio theory and communications. A lot of us did. We were encouraged to, in order to do our jobs better." As if not wanting to talk more about herself, she asked about the others and their sisters and friends.

Lillian described how Kate and her daughters had managed the farm with the help of German POWs, and how Annette and Bernie used volunteers from the women's Land Army to help with the orchard upstate. "College students, housewives, young women – some of them traveling up from the city – to help harvest peaches, pears, and apples. Hard workers, all of them. Annette said they couldn't have done it without their help."

They reminisced about the Victory gardens, the volunteers at the USO canteens, the rationing and drives, and then said how thankful they all were that those days were behind them. They went on to talk about popular movies and songs and their plans for the holidays.

But then over dessert, the conversation once more turned back to the war years, to the role of the nurses. Lillian mentioned some of the things Edna had told her. Over their visit to Kate's farm in July, she and Edna had sat up late talking one night.

"She had plenty of her own stories about D-Day, field hospitals, and barely escaping approaching tanks. But she also talked about the nurses she had trained with who served in Pearl Harbor, and the Philippines – the horror and cruelty they experienced. And their heroism."

Lillian had often mulled over something Edna had expressed that night and decided to share it. "One night, she told me of some particularly terrible things that had happened, things she had seen. And she said, 'My estimation of humanity has dropped, I'm sorry to say. I want to spend the rest of my life trying to get it back. To keep doing what I can to help the poor wounded world.'

And so, she works at a veteran's hospital nearby. I don't think anyone understands why she does it."

The table grew quiet and Mrs. Sullivan said, "I think the trauma has changed us all. Many of us want to look away, to look on something good and whole and promising. Hence the shopping, and marriages, and entertainment, and fashion. I feel it myself. It's overwhelming, what happened, the stories, the horror."

Izzy agreed. "I think we're all in a state of healing, and maybe that needs to be protected by isolating ourselves. Selfishly, perhaps, but honestly, how much can a person, or a nation, take?"

"But then we have that luxury, don't we," Claudia said softly. "So many countries are still in survival mode. Despair and desolation mode." She picked up her fork and took a bite of cake. "It's beyond me. It all eludes understanding."

Which led Lillian to talk about Mrs. Wilson and her decision to adopt.

"I've heard Red talk about that," said Izzy, "and he said it's no light task. He said those kids have been through, and seen, so much." She shook her head and kept to herself whatever details Red had told her. "Then there's the bureaucracy, the tangled politics, and the almost impossible logistics. The idea of rescuing a child is one thing. The reality, I'm afraid, is another. And yet there are organizations that are trying."

As if collectively, they shifted to some humorous stories and how they had welcomed some of the wartime challenges and opportunities.

"Chances are, I would still be a typist," said Izzy. "Because there were no men to fill the jobs, I went from typist, to office manager, to being Rockwell's right-hand man. I even found the courage at one point to quit. Then I trained as a welder, worked briefly in an office on gasoline fraud rationing, and returned to Rockwell Publishing on my terms, with a contract!" She gave a loud laugh. "How I found the nerve to do that I'll never know."

She lifted her sherry and said, "Those days are definitely gone. I have to watch my step now."

Lillian had to laugh at Izzy's description, but added, "Mr. Rockwell has always been completely dependent on you, Izzy. I'd say you'll be there for as long as you want to be."

Izzy raised her glass. "Here's hoping," she said, and took a sip.

Claudia was greatly impressed by all of their work paths, and related the excitement she felt working with the WAVES. "I met such interesting people, men and women. With a passion to do things, to make a difference, to become more. That's where I met Philip."

Izzy had heard bits and pieces over the years from Edith's letters. "And you're engaged?"

"We're – we've talked about marriage. He wants it. I – I'm not sure. I don't think there's a better man out there for me. But I'm afraid of –" it took her a while to find the right word – "of disappearing."

"But you have such fine examples of happy marriages," said Lillian, puzzled by her hesitation. "Your sisters, your brother."

"I know. My sisters are happy. I look at my sister-in-law, Susan, and her role as mother and wife, helpmate to Robert. I admire them and take comfort in them. But – for myself, I'm not sure. It's as if I can't see clearly or act decisively. During the war, I had such focus, such purpose. I was needed and I did my job well. Now – all that's changed, and I feel a bit adrift."

Mrs. Sullivan patted her arm. "To find the love of an honorable man is no small thing. But I also had the opportunity to test myself, to earn my way in the world, to be a part of something bigger. I do believe that everything that came before marrying Brendan has made our marriage even stronger."

"I can say the same for me and Red," said Izzy. "But you need to be clear on what matters to you most. I don't think it's wise to rush into anything, Claudia. You're still young. For the time being, you can have both work and romance. You've done it so far. Don't feel pressured to give up everything you've worked so hard on."

"No, I don't intend to," Claudia said firmly. Then in a more tentative manner, she added, "But, at the same time, I don't want to end up an old maid."

Mrs. Sullivan squared her shoulders on hearing that. "I was a very happy old maid, for quite some time. There's something to be said for a life of work. But then, I wasn't alone. I had my family and a busy role as an aunt. You have that too, Claudia." Mrs. Sullivan poured herself another cup of tea, added a splash of milk, and took a sip. "Take your time, dear. Let the world settle down a bit. Then perhaps you can see more clearly."

Claudia took in the words, nodding, but still looked doubtful.

"In the meantime," Lillian added, "continue on your path and listen to your heart. Only you know what will make you happy."

Claudia gave a short laugh. "Of that, I *am* clear."

And then the conversation had bounced back to the holidays, and caroling, and the upcoming Christmas parties.

But that underlying tension had stayed with Lillian. The stories of so many women that would never be heard – women who would never be painted, sculpted, or written about. They would be buried in the stories of others. Footnotes.

As she continued walking home, she had to ask herself if it was true for her as well. Was that what was really bothering her? She knew in her heart that her life as an artist was about to change. That the life she had so carefully carved out for herself could be gone in a minute.

She crossed into Central Park and headed for the broad expanse of the bench-lined Literary Walk. Its statues of poets and towering elms spoke of both art and beauty, which she found inspiring and comforting. She reminded herself that job or no job, the art would remain. The searching and yearning for beauty would always drive her, and fill her.

Lillian took one of the sidewalks that led to the beginning of the Walk. She had been deep in thought, walking with her head down. But when she lifted her head to see the falling snow, she stopped, and gave a soft "Ohh!" at the view before her.

All her worries disappeared, and she smiled out at the beauty, the wonder, the magic. A light snow had dusted the park and covered the tree limbs and benches. Oddly enough, the entire walk-way, usually full of people strolling, was empty. That wouldn't last long, she knew. She heard children playing and laughter and voices behind her.

But for a brief moment, the snow lay untram-meled, smooth, a white expanse softly aglow in the lamplights that had recently come on. She was humbled by such beauty, and it gave her a shake, as if reminding her of the larger view of life, that rising above the world and seeing its wonder. It was stirring and encouraging, as if it was on her side somehow. She was not alone with her woes anymore. She had the beauty of the world right at her fingertips, nudging her into a different frame of mind. Older, timeless, wiser.

She lingered another moment to take it all in – and was brought back to the here and now by the laughter and whoops of children. A group of boys and girls ran past her pulling a sled, and two more trailed behind in their own game, scooping up snow and tossing it into the air.

As she watched them frolic, she smiled and thought of her own children, and Charles, and dinner needing to be made, and she quickened her steps.

When she approached the end of the walkway, she crossed the road to stand above the Bethesda Plaza and paused to admire the scene before her. The steps and balustrade leading down to the plaza appeared architectural now, in crisp white lines. At the foot of them, the snow-ringed fountain stood alone in the white of the plaza.

Lillian gazed at the angel atop the fountain with its wings, hair, and outstretched arm highlighted in white. The woods on the other side of the lake formed a backdrop of lacey bare trees delicately outlined in white. She took a deep breath and let the day's beauty seep into her.

She decided she would come back sometime over the winter, after another snowfall, and bring her sketchpad. And a thermos of hot chocolate. For now, home.

Lillian followed the road and soon exited the park. Another few blocks and she was back in her neighborhood. Just as she was about to turn onto her street, a figure on the sidewalk caught her attention due to its unusual, exaggerated walk – big steps, bent forward, arms swinging. *Billy?* She broke into a silent laugh as she watched him round the corner, noting that people paused to watch him in wonder as he strode by.

She reached her apartment building and took the elevator. Tommy and Gabriel would have brought Charlotte home by now, and chances are she would be hungry. Or maybe not – Mrs. Kuntzman most likely fed her all day.

From the end of the hall, came sounds of scratchy music – Mrs. Taggert playing her old Victrola. Ah, Lillian thought, Bach. She remembered her girlhood days of struggling to play the Preludes on the piano. She was tempted to stand and listen to the beautiful strains of melody.

But the boys' laughter and Charlotte's babbling prompted her to open her door. Home. No better place to be. She draped her coat over the chair and quickly pulled off her gloves and tossed them aside, and then swooped down to Charlotte's raised arms and cries of "mama," and lifted her.

"My darling girl!" Lillian held her close and turned side to side, smiling at Tommy and Gabriel as they filled her in on how they picked her up at Mrs. Kuntzman's, and how Henry was there helping her with her baking. And how Mrs. Kuntzman insisted on giving them some of the chicken pot pie that was just coming out of the oven, and the stories Henry told them while they were eating it, and Charlotte needing to be changed one more time, and eating a few of the snickerdoodles she had just baked that afternoon.

"She gave us a bunch of them," said Gabriel. "We put them in the cookie tin."

"So, we just got home and aren't too hungry yet," added Tommy.

"Good," Lillian said, setting Charlotte back on the couch with the boys. "That gives me more time to get dinner ready. Let's have some music, Gabriel. See what you can find on the radio."

The apartment soon filled with music and laughter, mixed with sounds of sizzling, chopping, and humming coming from the kitchen. Within an hour, the table was set, and dinner was ready as Charles walked in the door.

He went through the same motions that Lillian had – scooping up Charlotte into his arms, listening to the boys' account of Henry and Mrs. Kuntzman, and then giving him a demonstration of Charlotte's wobbly toddling, balancing herself on her own, before collapsing. Charles then went into the kitchen and put his arm around Lillian and sniffed the air.

"Smells good." He took a sample of the hamburger steak and onions that she offered out of the pan. "Mmm. Very good." He poured himself a small whiskey and took a sip. "How was your lunch?"

"Just wonderful. It was so good to see them all." Lillian gave a brief recap.

Tommy came into the kitchen. "She's almost asleep, Mom. Should we put her in her crib?"

Gabriel carried Charlotte into the kitchen, whispering. "One minute she was laughing, and the next her eyes were closed. I think she must have played all day."

With a nod from Lillian, the boys gently laid her in the crib and then sat at the table.

The image of Billy popped into her mind. "Gabriel, I saw Billy on his way home – doing the most extraordinary walk."

"Oh, that's the George M. Cohan-walk. He's nailed it, Mom. With his hair brushed back in his checked cap, he looks just like James Cagney in *Yankee Doodle Dandy.*"

Charles shot a smile at Lillian. "I can't wait to see the performance. What's your role going to be, Gabriel – besides directing?"

"The song isn't very long, so we thought I could introduce it first. You know, say how George M. Cohan was given a medal by President Roosevelt in 1940. For his World War One songs. How much they boosted morale and helped with the war. In the movie, that's when Cagney says 'I'm just a song and dance man.' Billy really wanted to say those lines, but in the movie Cohan's old by then, so that doesn't fit. So basically, I'll introduce him. Then – he'll sing and dance! He's a good tap dancer. There's a part where Cagney kind of dances up a wall but the stage doesn't have a wall. So, Billy is going to do cartwheels instead."

Tommy groaned and took a bite of mashed potatoes.

Charles had to laugh. "You should be happy, Tommy. Isn't that better than both of them nursing at a she-wolf?" That set them all laughing – especially Tommy.

"So, you'll have a few lines on stage," said Lillian. "What will you wear? And what will Billy wear?"

"Well, for that song in the movie, Cagney is wearing a suit. So, Billy has an old suit he'll wear. It's kind of short on him, but Cagney's suit looks too short on him too. Mr. G is going to lend him a riding whip from the shop. I thought I could wear my gent's costume from Valentine's Day. Dusty suggested some glasses. He picked out a pair for me with round frames." Mimicking Dusty tapping his fingertips together, Gabriel added, "It will give me a professorial air."

"And how's the hauling business," asked Charles. "Staying busy?"

"We're raking in the dough. Delivering groceries, though Mr. Mancetti's still not sure it's a good idea. A few Christmas trees from the lot. Those people tip the most. A delivery for Mr. G from time to time – oh, and we might expand to rides."

"Rides!" cried Tommy. "Like a bus?" He looked from Charles to Lillian. "Can they do that? I mean, it is allowed?"

"Sure, it's allowed," answered Gabriel. "We gave Junior three rides from the Red String so far. We don't charge him, but it gave us the idea. The last time his friend Bessie joined him. Billy ran the last block and when he turned the corner they almost tumbled out. They said it was the most fun they'd had in years." Gabriel finished his milk and pushed back his chair.

"Can I go visit Mrs. Taggert? I want to ask if I can listen to her Victrola sometime. She has the 'Yankee Doodle Dandy' song and I'd like to listen to it. Get some ideas."

Lillian briefly pondered whether she should let him go, but Mrs. Taggert, who lived alone, enjoyed Gabriel's company. "Just for a few minutes. And bring her a few of Mrs. Kuntzman's cookies."

"Come with me Tommy. She always asks about you."

"I'm already getting her cookies," Tommy said, filling a small plate. "Let's go."

Before Lillian closed the cookie tin, both boys reached for a snickerdoodle and bit into them on their way out.

Chapter 11

Billy and Gabriel parked their wagon near the checkers table at the Red String Curio Store and sat among the group of regulars: Junior, still glowing from the invigorating ride the boys had given him; Dusty, who had declined their offer of a free demonstration; Henry, who said he would be more than happy to try out their services sometime; and Mr. G, who stood nearby, rocking on his heels, his twinkling eyes traveling from the conversation to the browsing customers, to the front door, and back to the group of friends.

"Gabriel," Henry said when the topic of rides was over, "I came across your friend Happy at the hospital yesterday. I was expecting the mild-mannered chap I remember from a year ago."

Gabriel looked uncertainly at Henry. "What do you mean?"

Henry gave a worried chuckle. "He wasn't happy yesterday. He came storming into the rec room, fuming mad, saying someone ratted on him.

Gave him away to the enemy. Took us a while to figure out what he was getting at." He shook his head. "I always said they let him go too early. Had some more healing to do."

"I never saw him like that. What happened?"

"Turns out one of the fellas told his brother where to find him in the park. He nearly fell apart telling us. He pulled on his beard and his raggedy coat and said, 'He saw me like *this*! I'll never be the same to him.' Then he went on about No Man's Land and…" Henry shook his head again. "Very sad. Then just as quickly, he stormed out."

Gabriel squinted at the table, trying to remember if he had told anyone about where Hap usually sat in the park. "I didn't tell anyone. Just my mom. But she wouldn't say anything. She said it's against the rules."

Henry kept his eyes on his hands, tapping them against his knees. "Well, maybe it is, maybe it is."

"But I tell people about the hot chocolate man and where his pushcart is. Maybe I accidentally said something about Hap, too."

Junior chimed in on seeing Gabriel's concern. "Most likely others saw him in the park. Surely you weren't the only one, Gabriel. Makes no sense."

"None at all," echoed Dusty. "Don't you fret. And who knows, maybe it's a good thing. Time will tell."

During the conversation, Billy had occupied himself with a wooden gadget that formed some kind of a puzzle. He finally gave up in exasperation and set it back on the table. "I can't figure this thing out. It would make a good gift for someone you don't like." He glanced out the window at the fading day. "Time to go, Gabe."

Gabriel perked up at this. "We have a big order at Mancetti's grocery store."

Billy recounted their success over the week. "Besides deliveries here and at Mancetti's, we delivered two Christmas trees, and gave three rides – a dime each. If it keeps up, I'll have enough to start classes right after Christmas." He lost some of his enthusiasm as he added, "As long as my parents let me. They think acting is a waste of time."

Mr. G rubbed his chin in thought. "Perhaps this school performance of yours will convince them otherwise. If you're truly serious about drama."

"Oh, I'm serious, all right." Billy sat up, turning Mr. G's words over in his mind. "Hmm. Show my parents what I got. Pull out all the stops."

"Well, that's not quite... " began Mr. G, but let his words drift off.

Junior massaged his arthritic hands and grinned at Billy's response. "That's one way of putting it."

"At any rate," said Henry, "we'll all be there, cheering you on!"

Mr. G nodded. "Indeed, we look forward to such jollity! We'll be sure to clap effusively and offer high praise to your teachers – and parents," he added with a wink. "We've seen you in action, so to speak, and believe in you whole-heartedly!"

"Gee, thanks!" said Billy, his face full of hope. "Things are looking up! Come on, Gabe – duty calls!"

As they made their way to Mancetti's, the two boys discussed painting a sign for the wagon listing their various services: hauling, deliveries, and rides, under the name of the business. They had narrowed it down to Hercules Hauling and B&G Professional Transport.

"Maybe we could add some cushions for the rides," said Gabriel. "Make it more comfortable."

"Junior didn't seem to mind. Or Bessie."

Their minds often working in tandem, the two boys broke into a spontaneous replay of the other day with Junior and his friend.

Gabriel sat primly in the wagon while Billy began to pull the wagon at a run. In imitation of Junior, Billy cried out, "Hold on to your hat, Bessie!" and Gabriel shrieked in delight, with his hand atop his cap.

They arrived at Mancetti's right on time, and Tommy and Mr. Mancetti were soon loading up the wagon. They carefully arranged two bottles of milk, a carton of eggs, a box of potatoes, carrots, onions, and some canned vegetables. A bag of flour and a small sack of apples topped the load. Mr. Mancetti gave them strict instructions on how and where to make the delivery.

His face creased in doubt as Tommy read off the list and Billy answered in some kind of wise guy character: "Check! We got dat! Apples? We got dem, too. Flour? Check!"

Gabriel gave Billy a nudge when he saw Mr. Mancetti's worried face.

"Now, Billy," Mr. Mancetti said. "These are to be delivered in a professional manner. No horse-play."

Billy straightened his shoulders and dropped the act. "Don't worry, Mr. Mancetti. We're serious businessmen. We'll deliver this load and be back in a jiffy. In time for another delivery, if you like."

"Hmm." Mr. Mancetti scratched his cheek and twisted his mouth to one side, doubt all over his face. Then he waved his arm at the boys. "All right, then. Off you go."

Tommy shot Gabriel a warning look and whispered, "This is one of his best customers, Gabriel. Be professional."

"Check," answered Gabriel.

When the two boys turned the corner, Billy looked at Gabriel and rolled his eyes. "Worried about a bunch of vegetables. What could go wrong? Come on. Let's deliver this and go to the Christmas tree lot on the way back. Maybe we can squeeze in another delivery before going back to the store."

They checked the address and hurried along, talking about the "Yankee Doodle Dandy" song and dance act, which customers tipped the best, and which of their services was the most fun to do.

"Christmas stuff is the best for tips," said Gabriel. "The rides, for sure, are the most fun."

They exchanged looks again, smiled, and Billy cried, "Hold on to your hat, Bessie!" And they took off running, Billy pulling the wagon and Gabriel steadying the merchandise.

"Slow down, Billy!" Gabriel cried, laughing as they rounded a corner. "Watch out!" he screamed, at the sudden appearance of a workman carrying a ladder into a building.

Gabriel lunged to anchor the groceries on top, tripping over Billy's feet, but the wagon fishtailed, and then turned onto two wheels, and then – "

Silence, as they stared at the disaster before them, the wagon on its side, both boys on the sidewalk, dusted with flour. In their attempt to catch the falling items, they had only made it worse – punching the flour bag open, ensuring that all the eggs got broken, and sending the potatoes and onions rolling into the street. They looked at the mess and then at each other.

"Oh, no!"

"We're in big trouble."

One uncracked milk bottle made a light gurgling sound as the last of the milk escaped.

Billy looked at it. "I *won't* cry over spilled milk. I *won't* cry over spilled milk. I *won't* – "

His chant was interrupted by a loud "Hey!" Coming from the other direction was a group of four boys. The youngest one ran ahead and stopped at the mess. "Hey! That's my wagon!" He turned to the oldest boy. "Teddy! Look! My wagon."

Gabriel turned to Billy. "I thought you said it was abandoned."

The group of boys inspected the wagon. The one who was Teddy checked the painted suns on the side. "This belongs to my kid brother! You stole it?"

Billy shook his head and jumped to his feet. "No! I found it in the park. It was abandoned!"

Teddy took off his cap and swatted his little brother with it. "How many times I gotta tell you not to leave it there?"

"The wheel was broken and I couldn't pull it, then when I went back with Monty to get it, I couldn't find it."

Billy brushed at the flour on his pants. "I paid to get that broken wheel fixed. It's good as new now."

"Gee, thanks!" said the boy.

One of the other boys righted the wagon and tested the wheels. "No harm done, Teddy. Other than the mess covering it."

Teddy thumped his finger on Billy's chest. "Next time, don't take what's not yours." He looked at the potatoes and onions, the broken glass and spilled milk, and shook his head. He reached for a few apples and handed them to the other boys. Then to Billy and Gabriel: "You better get this mess cleaned up. Before someone calls the cops on you." He leaned into Billy's face and took a loud crunch of the apple before leaving.

Gabriel and Billy watched them walk off, seeing Teddy give another light swat to his little brother, before putting his arm around him.

With his eyes fixed on the group and the wagon, Gabriel shook his head. "There goes our business."

"There goes my classes," said Billy.

From the same building where the workman had gone in, the super came out with a trash can, a broom, and a large metal dustpan. "Better get this cleaned up, boys."

"Thanks," said Gabriel, getting to his feet. "Want an apple?" He picked one up, rubbed it on his jacket, and held it out.

"Don't mind if I do." The super bit into the apple and planted himself on the stairs to enjoy the show.

Gabriel took the broom and gathered up the broken glass.

Billy took the dustpan and tried to scoop up the eggy mess, then watched it ooze off the dustpan as he held it over the garbage can.

When the worst was in the trash can, they picked up a few salvageable cans. They lifted the hems of their coats to form pouches, and filled them with the cans, vegetables, and a few remaining apples. Then they began their slow trek back to Mancetti's, bracing themselves for a storm.

Chapter 12

Izzy, wearing a new loden green suit and a stylish black cashmere coat, cheerfully entered Rockwell Publishing. Her hair was freshly cut and styled, and she wore a brighter shade of lipstick – all from the shopping spree with her sister, Lois. Two new suits, three office dresses, a new coat, and a new pair of shoes. The longer hems, richer fabrics, and fashionable touches were all a delight. The restrictive austerity of the war years was behind them. Her sister was right – with so many choices and with hope and happiness in the air, it was quite an easy thing to become an enthusiastic consumer. Good for the economy? She would do her part!

Part of Izzy's optimism stemmed from her decision to commit to her old job – no more doubts about which path to take. Like her old suits, the family construction business was history. No more dreadfully boring Saturdays! A new, exciting life with Red. He would finish up on the GI Bill and find work that brought him happiness.

She smiled up at the Christmas tree in the lobby, festooned with tinsel garlands and sparkling red, silver, and gold ornaments. Ah, the Christmas season! Even her new black suede pumps clicking against the marble floor brought her pleasure.

She loved her job, loved the role she had carved out for herself, even loved the troublesome Mr. Rockwell and his glittery wife. She was looking forward to the Christmas party later in the day that she had helped plan, along with Mrs. Rockwell.

Twelve years of working at this job. It had been difficult, trying, at times she had wanted to pull her hair out at Rockwell's petty demands. But he had also promoted her, and allowed her to develop the position to suit her, and she was grateful.

Yes, she was one of the lucky ones! she thought, as she smiled to everyone in the elevator.

*

Claudia sat at the small desk in her room, going through job applications. She had completed her degree with high marks and had relevant experience working with the WAVES – two whole years. This was New York City, she kept telling herself. She *would* find work. She was sure of it.

Yes, it would be an uphill battle, as Robert was fond of telling her. But then, going uphill strengthens the heart, the body – as long as one perseveres. The WAVES had taught her to be diligent, responsible, hard-working, and committed. Wherever she worked, she would give it her all.

She *had* to be a part of something larger, devote herself to some worthy purpose. And if I become an old maid, she thought, I'll be the happiest one that ever was. The war years had taught her how to be tough and courageous, how to believe in herself, and how to push herself to be more. She gave a firm nod and reached for the third application.

She pushed down the memory of her break with Philip. It had been thrilling working with him at the Naval Communications Office. The collaboration, the discussions, the late nights working on finding solutions, discussing new ideas. She looked out the window at the falling snow. But to be honest, once the job was over, the thrill was also over. She discovered that outside of work, she and Philip had very little in common. Certainly not enough to fill a lifetime. She was sad, disappointed – and relieved.

From downstairs, the laughter of her family filled the air. She winced. Robert would be upset at her decision about Philip – but he would come round, once he saw how happy she was soon to be. Wouldn't he?

She couldn't help feeling that the world was opening up to her, instead of closing in. She would write to Edith about her decision. Over the summer on her visit, Edith had casually mentioned that Claudia should visit her and Desmond, stay a while and look around. Perhaps find a job. At the time, it had sounded like a welcome possibility. But privately, Edith had also mentioned that she and Desmond missed New York City, and might move back in a year or two.

Claudia held up the last job form, and thought – No. I'm on my own in this. I need to make it work for me here, now. Her eyes brightened in determination as she filled out the application.

*

Charles stood rooted to the floor, unable to believe his ears. Eric Clay was actually chastising Mrs. Sullivan for going out to lunch twice in one week. As if it was any of his business. As if there was anything wrong with it! And alluding to her age. What nerve! Why, she was a better worker than ten of him. A hundred!

There was Mrs. Sullivan, fists on her hips, firmly holding her ground against his charges. But should she have to? Should any of his employees have to put up with that?

He had heard enough. "Mr. Clay! In my office. Now."

The bully cowed at having been caught.

Mrs. Sullivan gave a short nod of thanks to Mr. Drooms, and, ever the professional, simply continued with her work. Her whole body flooded with relief and she realized how tense she had become of late.

At the end of day, Charles went to speak to Mrs. Sullivan and told her that Mr. Clay would be leaving, and most likely taking Mr. Creeley with him. "He told me 'they didn't need this lousy joint.'"

"Thank goodness for that!" said Mrs. Sullivan. "There will be rejoicing among the staff."

"As bad as all that?" When Charles pressed her for more details, she gave him several examples, in particular, "with the younger gals in the office."

He suddenly remembered the day Miss Wynn left the office crying and asked if she was one of them.

"She was his favorite target. He knew she didn't have a husband or beau and berated her for it. He felt safe tormenting her."

"But why didn't she speak up about it?" Charles asked.

"She couldn't risk losing her job. She's the sole supporter of her family."

"Mrs. Sullivan, you know my work ethic and what I expect of my employees. If anything like that ever happens again, you must let me know."

She opened her mouth to speak, but then decided against it, and simply nodded.

In a flash, Charles remembered that she had said something about it. And he had brushed it off, saying they would work it out between them. He gave a defeated smile. "You *did* speak to me and you are too high-minded to remind me of it. I remember now. I'm sorry I didn't listen."

Mrs. Sullivan shook her head at the thought. "You were extremely busy that day, sir, and I picked the wrong time to tell you. I'm afraid my temper got the better of me."

And now she's making excuses for me, Charles thought. "We never got around to reinstating our weekly update meetings. Let's go back to doing that. It worked well for us in the past."

"Gladly, sir." She began to take her leave.

"Mrs. Sullivan, you're planning the office Christmas party, aren't you? Why don't you ask Miss Wynn to be your special deputy. At my request."

Privately, Charles decided to increase the young woman's salary, possibly redefine her role. She had been one of those quiet, persevering employees, never complaining. Near invisible, but indispensable. He would discuss the staff with Mason and Mrs. Sullivan, and make sure he wasn't missing anything else. They had always worked best as a team, the three of them. He was glad to have them both at his side again.

*

Lillian filled with excitement. Mr. Borland had just announced that the series was hers, though a few changes would have to be made to the designs. A hint of a salary increase was also made.

The series of women in the workforce was hers! Surely, this was the culmination of her career – what more could she ask for? She couldn't wait to tell Charles that the celebration was on!

Once the meeting was over, and the others had left the room, she asked Mr. Borland if she would be working on it with Mrs. Huntington.

Mr. Borland cast his eyes down as he shuffled a stack of papers. "For personal reasons, Mrs. Huntington has decided to leave the company. I think she's looking forward to retirement." He looked up. "You'll be reporting to me."

"I see," said Lillian, trying her best to remain composed.

Mr. Borland's secretary came into the conference room at that moment with her steno pad, and Lillian quietly left. She took the stairs two floors down and walked hurriedly down the corridor to Mrs. Huntington's desk.

There she was, packing a small box with items from her desk drawers. She looked up at Lillian and gave a wry smile. "You heard the news."

Lillian nodded.

"There's not much to pack. I already brought most of it home. Still, it came sooner than I thought. I assumed I had until the new year."

Lillian felt a crushing sense of defeat. "What will you do? Is this – retirement?"

"Retirement! Is that what he told you? He knows me well enough to guess that I have something else. I've been working on other possibilities for the past few months. I could see what was in store for me."

"You've found another job?"

"More like I helped to create another job. I recently met with an old colleague of mine. He and his wife have been wanting to open up their own design firm. Now that the war's over and things are looking up, they've decided to do it. And they want me to head it up. They've already secured a location down in the Village." She took a deep breath and held it for a moment. Then let it out. "I'm quite excited about it. To be starting over at this time of life is going to be a challenge, but I'm up for it."

Lillian helped her tuck the corners of the box in. "I'm sure you'll make a success of it."

Mrs. Huntington gave a soft smile at Lillian's disappointment. "It goes without saying, Lillian, that I would love to have you with us. The work will be exciting. But we couldn't pay anything near what Mr. Borland can. I think he's worried that I'll somehow take you away."

"He's offered me the series."

Mrs. Huntington merely nodded. "I thought he would. With a raise?"

Lillian gave a small nod. "He hinted at it."

"If he was really smart, he would have done more than hint. His strategy will be to string you along for as long as he can." She gave a light shake of her head, then put her attention back on Lillian. "Listen. Though I would love nothing more than to continue our collaboration, you must do what's right for you. As a professional, I have to tell you that this series will be a real feather in your cap. It will increase your marketability for years to come. It will cement your reputation."

"And on a personal level?" asked Lillian.

"Oh. Well, that's another matter entirely, isn't it? Only you can answer that question."

"Without you here, everything will change. Mr. Borland hinted at *improvements* to my work that I'm not sure I want to make."

Mrs. Huntington leaned against her desk and looked at Lillian.

"To play devil's advocate, book covers must sell. That's their purpose. And there's a bundle to be made. Mr. Borland, and the company, I might add, are in step with the times. They want to depict women in the house – or manor," she added with a laugh. "Beauty, romance, and tradition. Wives and mothers. The idealization of the domestic life. That's what the market demands now. For authors, as well. Many of whom are women. But bear in mind, Lillian, that sometimes the content they write is not so – submissive. Though the covers might suggest otherwise."

"I see." Lillian added this bit of information to everything else and was left feeling confused, dispirited, and feeling that from now on she would be less in control of her work.

Mrs. Huntington took a pencil and piece of paper from the desk next to hers and wrote down an address. "Stop by. We'll have lunch together and I'll show you my new workplace and introduce you to my friends. And I'll do my darndest to convince you to come work for us. Next month, next year, whenever the time is right for you."

Lillian looked at the address and slipped it into her purse.

Mrs. Huntington placed a hand on Lillian's arm. "It's no light thing to be given the covers. Whatever they depict. At least he recognizes talent. I'll give him that."

They said their goodbyes and Lillian promised to stop by in a week or so.

Outside, the sky was heavy with dark troubled clouds, mirroring her state of mind. Lillian took the cross-town bus and then slowly walked home, filled with a sense of sadness at the departure of Mrs. Huntington.

Feeling nostalgic for former days, Lillian decided to turn onto her old street. Her spirits lifted somewhat on seeing her old neighbors, Mrs. Kinney standing outside her brownstone, talking with Mrs. Wilson.

Mrs. Kinney saw Lillian and waved. "Hello, Lillian! So nice to see you." With an expression both disapproving and amused, she announced: "Billy and Gabriel are on their way to pay Mr. Mancetti what they owe him and to help out at the store for a few hours to make up for his loss. I guess that's the end of their transport business. And Billy's so-called acting career."

Lillian felt an unexpected sense of loss on Billy's behalf. "Well, Billy does have a certain – talent."

"That's what I was just saying," Mrs. Wilson added. "When my boys were young and they hankered after something, I often gave in. I found that was the quickest way to get it out of their systems."

Lillian smiled at the tactic, but noticed that Mrs. Wilson's demeanor lacked enthusiasm. She seemed tired, disheartened.

Lillian turned to Mrs. Kinney. "I think classes might be a good thing for Billy. A good discipline. He'll get a real taste of the work involved. He'll either love it or grow tired of it."

"And move on to something else," added Mrs. Wilson. "That's what happened with my boys."

Mrs. Kinney gave a sigh. "You may be right." Then she brightened and nudged Mrs. Wilson. "Go ahead. Tell Lillian your news."

Lillian's posture straightened in anticipation. Mrs. Wilson must have found a new job, or was rehired at her old one, or perhaps she had made headway in her idea of adoption.

Mrs. Wilson gave a weak smile. "Oh, my news. My oldest son and his wife are expecting. Finally. They're moving back to the city so that I can help out. I'll be a grandmother."

Lillian was unsure how to respond to the flat undertone. "How exciting! That's wonderful news."

Mrs. Kinney gave a firm nod. "You'll be busy now. No need to go looking for anything else."

"No, no need at all. I couldn't be happier. I'll have to get out my knitting needles!" Mrs. Wilson said with a forced laugh.

Mrs. Kinney glanced at the darkening sky. "Well, ladies, time to get dinner started. Good seeing you both," she said, and climbed the steps to her brownstone.

Lillian could see that the light had gone out of Mrs. Wilson. "I guess this means you won't be adopting. You'll be busy with a baby soon." She was alarmed to see tears form in the older woman's eyes.

Mrs. Wilson spoke in a voice filled with loss, and appeared utterly forlorn. "I had my heart set on it. All the things we were going to do. I was going to make her so happy. I –" She looked down, and swallowed. "I can't shake the feeling that I'm abandoning a little girl in braids somewhere." She took a shaky breath and pulled a hankie from her pocket and dabbed her eyes, blew her nose. "I know I'm being foolish. Harry said we're too old anyway." She let a few moments go by. "Maybe I'm just upset that the doors are now closed for me, at this stage of my life."

"Oh, that's not true!" Lillian said, trying to inject some lightness. "You'll be a wonderful grandmother! And such a help to your son and his wife."

Mrs. Wilson nodded. "Mmm. It will be nice to have them close. After all these years. And of course, I'll enjoy the baby. What could be sweeter?" The suppressed anguish in her voice revealed her despair.

Lillian offered a few encouraging words and spoke about Charlotte and babyhood in general, the joy it brought. Then they said goodbye and promised to meet again soon.

Lillian walked home, selfishly happy that she was not at 'that stage' of life. That her children were still young and at home and needed her. That she had her own baby, her work, a loving husband… She took a hankie out of her pocket and wondered why she was so upset.

She hoped that whatever Mrs. Wilson was feeling wasn't waiting for her as well, in a couple of years. She hoped the boys wouldn't move away or be killed in a war…

She picked up her pace. She wanted to be home, surrounded by her things, her family.

Tommy would have picked up Charlotte from Mrs. Kuntzman by now, Charles would be home after work, Gabriel would be home for dinner. She was surprised at her need, the visceral need, to hold Charlotte, to see Tommy, to hear Gabriel's account of his day, to feel Charles's arms around her.

*

After Gabriel and Billy paid Mr. Mancetti for the spilled groceries, swept his shop and helped unpack some boxes with Tommy, they walked over to Central Park. They headed south and slowly made their way down to the entrance near 59th Street. This part of the park was always lively, even in the cold, and it felt good to be around a lot of people – people who had never heard of Hercules Hauling or whatever they would have called their business.

They sat down on an empty bench. Billy put his elbows on his knees, his head in his hands, eyes on the ground.

But Gabriel took in the vibrancy all around him – the honking traffic, all the people inside the park. He saw several soldiers – some were posing for photographs, others were laughing with a couple of girls. Three sailors bought hot pretzels from a street vendor and then stopped to watch a chess match between two old men. There were kids playing – one boy walked a dog that was bigger than him, two girls sang along to their hand-clapping game. There were nannies talking together as they pushed baby carriages or rested on benches, several couples strolling arm in arm, and people lined up to buy hot dogs and roasted peanuts.

Gabriel stuck his hands in his pockets, found a few coins, and counted them. He gave a big smile and elbowed Billy.

"I got just enough for some roasted peanuts or a hot chocolate. What'll it be?"

"You decide," said Billy, his eyes still on the ground.

Gabriel decided on a hot chocolate. He chatted with the vendor for a bit, asking him how business was. He took a sip. "Pretty good!" he said, and waved goodbye.

Then he sat next to Billy and offered him the cup. They each took a few sips.

"Look around you, Billy. This is New York City! There must be thousands of jobs, just waiting to be filled."

When that didn't get a response from Billy, he tried a different approach. "We could ask Mr. G to be on the lookout for another wagon. He could easily find one for us."

Billy turned down his mouth. "Nah. I've kind of lost my taste for the transport business."

Gabriel thought of the playground nearby. "We could go swing."

After a few more minutes of silence, Gabriel took yet another approach. He wasn't giving up. "So, let's keep our eye on the ball, Billy. The real reason for the wagon was to help with your acting career. That's the important thing, right? We have the skit. We're the grand finale. We have to make it good because it *will* go on your acting sheet. And you *will* have an acting career, one way or another."

Billy lightened up a little bit. "Thanks, pal. You're right."

Gabriel offered him the last sip of hot chocolate, and then tossed the cup into the garbage can. He sat back down next to Billy and saw that a shift had taken place in him.

Billy was now sitting up tall, turning something over in his mind. After a few more moments, his eyes began to fill with merriment, and a mischievous smile played about his mouth. "Hey. Gabriel."

A similar sly smile appeared on Gabriel's face. He recognized Billy's tone and knew exactly what it meant. Doing something that they shouldn't be doing. Something they could get in trouble for – but it would be oh so worth it.

"Yeah?"

"Is that a yes?" Billy asked.

"Most likely. What do you have in mind?"

"Our act. The song and dance." Billy bit his bottom lip and gave a chuckle. "Want to ham it up?"

Gabriel's eyes lit up at the words. "You don't mean at rehearsal, do you."

"Nope."

"You mean at the actual performance. When it would be too late to stop us."

"Yep."

Gabriel stood in front of Billy, cleared his throat, let his shoulders droop, and pushed up imaginary glasses. He began in a monotone voice:

'*Four score and seven years ago*' – he slowly nodded off, woke himself up with a snore, and gave himself a shake. Then he stood full of energy. "Just kidding, folks! For the grand finale, you will now see Billy Kinney as James Cagney as George M. Cohan singing 'Yankee Doodle Dandy!' Then blah, blah, blah congressional gold medal – and Take it away, Billy boy!"

Billy jumped to his feet and began talk-singing a few lines, Cagney style. "*I'm the kid that's all the candy, I'm a Yankee Doodle Dandy. I'm glad I am.*"

"*So's Uncle Sam!*" sang Gabriel, throwing his hands out rhythmically. "For the chorus, I'll pop out from behind the curtain, or under the curtain, and sing and dance my lines."

"Can you do cartwheels?"

"I can certainly try," replied Gabriel, indicating a performance in itself.

For the next half hour, they sang and danced, and hammed it up to their heart's content, combining dance moves from whatever entered their heads – farcical ballet leaps and twirls, the Three Stooges dance acts, and some entirely impromptu moves of their own. Sometimes they linked elbows, sometimes they sang and danced around a few stunned passersby.

They soon had a crowd around them of soldiers, young couples, and children freely laughing, and others asking questions: "Is that 'Yankee Doodle?' Are you actors? Do your mothers know you're here?" To which they answered *yes* or *no*, followed by, '*And that ain't no josh – we're Yankees, by gosh!*'

Some spectators left with their heads shaking, others laughed and clapped and waited for more.

When a soldier reached into his pocket and asked, "Were's your hat, kid?" Gabriel took Billy's cap from his head and tossed it out in front of them, and they started up all over again, introducing new moves, and new lines. Gabriel substituted "snickerdoodle" for "Yankee doodle," sending Billy into peals of laughter and inspiring him to new heights of improvisation. They kept at it until the day began to grow dim and the crowd finally thinned.

The boys dropped onto the bench, huffing. Gabriel lay back and laughed up at the sky. "Whew! That was our rehearsal for the grand finale!"

Billy gathered up his hat and counted the coins. A look of disbelief filled his face. "Gabriel! A dollar twenty-five!"

Gabriel sat up. "For *that*?"

Billy gave him a playful elbow in the side. "Who needs an old wagon? We can do this instead!"

"It doesn't feel like work at all."

They fell into laughter again at the unexpected hilarity of it all.

"Come on, pal," said Billy. "Let's go home."

Gabriel stood up to go. "In the meantime, let's keep this quiet. They might try to – you know – rein us in."

"Tone us down," added Billy. "Pour water on our fire. Or even cancel our act! Okay, Gabe. Until after the program, not a word. For now, we'll be serious."

"Oh, so serious."

And the two friends left the park with their arms slung over the other's shoulder, breaking into laughter now and then.

Chapter 13

Though the sweet smell of baking filled Lillian's kitchen, the usually happy scent got lost in the dark news that filled her mind. Up, down, up then down. That seemed to be her mind frame of late.

She pushed the newspaper away from her and stared at the floor, overwhelmed by the ongoing troubles of the world. The Nuremberg Trial and other horrors still pouring in, massive suffering and starvation, upheavals seemingly everywhere.

The war is over, she kept telling herself. Perhaps these regional problems would sort themselves out. No. She could no longer lie to herself. She had lived through two world wars, and she wasn't even old. There would be more wars, ever more wars.

Once a week she saw the results of warfare at the hospital. Some of the men – many of them – would never fully recover. Besides the wounded, a great number of them suffered in other ways. Lack of housing and jobs. Some had even resorted to begging. She thought of Hap Coleman and the account she had heard of him storming into the rec room, furious. How thin and disheveled and wild-eyed he had looked, how –

The doorbell rang, interrupting her thoughts, for which she was grateful. She glanced over at Charlotte who was stacking her alphabet blocks. "Who could that be?" Lillian said out loud. She pressed the buzz-in button. "I bet it's the package from my sister. Presents for you all!" She lifted Charlotte and went to the door with her, looking towards the elevator.

When the elevator door opened, out stepped Izzy. "Hello, Lillian."

"Izzy!" Lillian cried. "What a surprise!" All shadows and darkness vanished as she gave her friend a hug.

Izzy opened her arms to Charlotte. "Come to your Aunt Izzy. My, you have grown, haven't you?"

Charlotte babbled something that Izzy took for an answer, and kissed her cheek. "What a smart girl you are!" Over her shoulder she said to Lillian, "I had an appointment and left work early. Thought I'd stop by. I was hoping you were home."

Lillian turned on the kettle and got out cups and plates while Izzy took off her coat and walked around with Charlotte, commenting on the Christmas decorations.

"Your place is beautiful! I might have known you would make it magical. Just look at that tree! And your fireplace – it's gorgeous." Charlotte soon wriggled free and toddled back to her toys.

"If you stay long enough, you can see it when the tree lights are on. That's when it really looks magical. I just made a coffee cake – still warm."

The two friends were soon sitting at the kitchen table, like they used to. Different kitchen, different places in their lives. Same old friends, delighting in each other's company.

"Where are the boys?" Izzy asked, taking a whiff of the fresh coffee and cake placed before her and giving a sigh of enjoyment.

"They're going straight from their jobs to Mickey's for a Scouts meeting. His father is taking them caroling this evening to the hospitals. Then over to the diner for a Christmas celebration. They're so excited." She offered Izzy the sugar bowl and creamer.

"Good, good for them," said Izzy.

Lillian had the impression that Izzy was distracted. "So, you just left work early for an appointment? I don't remember you ever doing that before. Did Mr. Rockwell say anything?"

"Not a word. Funny," said Izzy, stirring in some sugar. "I actually never thought of doing it before. He didn't so much as blink."

There was definitely something different about Izzy. Lillian was sure she was preoccupied with something. They chatted about the kids, their sisters, plans for the holidays, with Lillian wondering if perhaps she was mistaken, and Izzy had indeed just stopped by for a spontaneous visit.

"How's Red?" Lillian asked, taking a bite of cake.

Izzy inclined her head. "He's doing all right, I think. It's been an adjustment for him. He was away for so long." She poured a splash of milk into her cup, perhaps forgetting that she had already done so, and stirred it, lost in her thoughts. She set her spoon down, and lifted her cup. "It was hard, wasn't it? Having them gone. Not knowing. Sometimes I wake up at night and reach out to touch him. Or I lean in close to hear his breathing. I feel like I've been given a gift, to have him back, and I want to keep checking that it's all true."

"I know what you mean. I do the same thing. Sometimes, after Charles leaves for work, I go to the window to catch a glimpse of him down on the sidewalk. It's like I want more of him."

Izzy gave a soft laugh and took a sip of coffee. "Do you think they do that?"

"Hmm. No, I don't think so. I think – it's different for them. One way is not better than the other – but it's different. I think they're more focused, in a way. On whatever's in front of them. At least, Charles is that way. His work takes up a lot of him."

Izzy nodded. "How's your work going?"

Lillian was soon telling Izzy about her situation with her job. "It's really caught me off guard. I was so thrilled to know that I would be doing the series. But I don't know what it will mean. Now that Mrs. Huntington has left."

"But she encouraged you to stay?"

"In a manner, from a professional perspective. She said it would be good for my long-term reputation."

"But she also asked you to go with her. And you don't know what that will mean, either. A new company could fold in a year. That's a tough one, Lilly. You've worked so hard to get where you are." Izzy leaned back in her chair, with a faraway look in her eye. "It's a hard thing to give up something you love. I'd give it some time. See how things go. You said yourself that you don't want any more changes."

Lillian held her cup in both hands as she considered Izzy's words. "I suppose that's the sensible thing to do. But it doesn't *feel* right." She took a sip of coffee and frowned. "I envy you, Izzy. Your path is clear. You've earned a solid place with Rockwell. He relies on you. You'll probably be there for another ten years or more."

Izzy gave a wry smile, took another sip of coffee, and slowly set the cup in the saucer. "Or at least for the next three or four months."

Lillian tipped her head at Izzy's words. "And then what? What will happen in three or four months?"

"I'll be showing."

Lillian froze with her mouth open. When Izzy nodded, tears shot to Lillian's eyes. She jumped up and held her friend. "Izzy! I'm so happy! I thought – I was beginning to think – that…"

Izzy shrugged. "So did I. After all this time, I thought we couldn't have children. But the doctor confirmed it today. I came straight here. I haven't even told Red yet. I'll tell him in person, tonight."

"He'll be so happy! And – everything is fine?" Lillian sat back in her chair, scooting it closer towards Izzy.

"I'm a little old to be having my first child – listen to me! Like I'm going to have a brood." Izzy held her head. "Oh, Lilly. I'm not afraid of the physical part. Well, maybe a little. But I'm not so sure about motherhood. I mean, I don't think I'll be very good at it."

"Of course, you will, Izzy! Look how you are with your nieces and nephews."

"I don't see them all that often. I love them, but I'm always glad to return home. It's exhausting."

"And look how you are with my kids. They adore you!"

"I'm a visiting aunt. That's all I've ever had to be. The idea of being responsible for a little person terrifies me."

Lillian laughed. "That will all disappear the moment you hold your baby in your arms. You'll be flooded with an almost overwhelming love. And joy."

"That's what my sis always says. That it's a different kind of love."

"It is. It's a love that goes to the core of you, powerful, yet humbling, so sweet and tender – it's hard to explain. One moment you're a ferocious mother bear, protecting her young. The next, you doubt your every move, worrying that you're missing something critical. Are they breathing? What is it they want? Why don't I know?" Lillian laughed at the memories of her motherhood. "But one thing is certain, Izzy. It will change you like nothing else. In the most profound way."

Izzy gave a deep sigh, but remained skeptical. "I know Red will be happy. I think – I think it will help him. He's had a hard time, you know." Izzy gave another groan. "We're going to have to rethink everything. A place. Red will have to find a job sooner than we thought. I hope – I hope it's not too much for him. He's…"

"It will all work out, Izzy. Don't worry. And I'll get to be the auntie to your little one."

Izzy's eyes filled with tears. "Forget the little one. *I'm* going to need your help, Lilly. Promise you'll be there for me."

Lillian laughed and hugged Izzy. "You'll have to push me away."

Izzy raised her tear-stained face. "Oh Lilly, let's meet more often, like we used to. Let's go to that café we used to go to. See if that old waitress is still there. Remember her? I'm sure she's gone. But wouldn't it be fun? Like old times?"

Lillian reached out to Izzy's hand, giving it a squeeze. "Of course, we will! I would love it too. Those were good days, Izzy. They really were. Even when I complained about them. Looking back, I loved it all. And don't worry about your life changing too much. Look at me – I had a baby later in life, and I still work and get out. Not as much, perhaps, but I still do. You will too, Izzy."

Izzy nodded, wanting to believe the words, but her eyes darted around in anxiety. "My life is about to change. I'm so fearful of giving up that old way. It's who I am. It's all I know."

"You're worrying for nothing, Izzy. You'll see." She had to smile at the doubt in her normally formidable friend's eyes. "Come to the kids' school program this weekend. We'll go out to dinner afterwards. While we still can," she added with a laugh.

"Billy as James Cagney singing 'Yankee Doodle Dandy?' I wouldn't miss it for the world!"

"Complete with cartwheels, I hear."

Izzy gave a laugh and finally relaxed a bit. "If anyone can cheer me up, it's that kid. We'd love to come. Life goes on, doesn't it. Changes come and we make the best of them." She took a deep breath and flashed a smile.

Lillian topped up their coffee. She saw that Izzy's vulnerability had finally disappeared and was replaced by the old meet-life-head-on Izzy.

Izzy smacked her forehead and gave a playful groan. "Oh! I bought the most beautiful new suits and dresses when Lois was here. I'll barely have the chance to wear them. By the time I can, the fashions will have changed."

Just then, sounds from down the hall changed the tone of everything – four boys laughing, arguing, running, and then bursting into the apartment. Tommy and Mickey entered, followed by Gabriel and Billy.

"Mom!" cried Tommy. "Oh, hi Miss Izzy! I mean, Mrs. McCann."

"I'll always be Izzy to you, Tommy. I mean, Tom."

"I thought you were going straight to Mickey's," said Lillian, "for the caroling."

"We have to tell you something first," said Tommy. "Go ahead, Gabriel. You go first."

Gabriel stood next to Lillian's chair and bracketed his hands, capturing her full attention. "Guess who came into the Red String to say goodbye?"

Lillian looked around, trying to think, then shook her head.

"Hap! He was with his brother. He found Hap in the park. They're going upstate to live on the farm. His brother's real nice. He's a teacher and in the summer, he helps out on the farm. He said there's plenty of work for Hap too, if he wants. And there's an extra bedroom for him. He said it's peaceful there, and quiet."

"That's wonderful!" said Lillian.

"And there are other vets up there who work on the farms. Hap looked completely different, all cleaned up. I thought he was an old guy, but he isn't. I told him my aunt has an orchard upstate and that maybe I would see him up there sometime."

Tommy looked puzzled, as if he just thought of something. "How did his brother find him in the park? It's so big."

"He said someone from the hospital sent his brother an anonymous letter. And told him where to go."

Izzy gave Lillian a side glance.

Lillian looked down at her coffee cup and turned it around. "Someone must have said something to someone…"

Izzy hid her smile at the vague response.

"It's a good thing they did," said Gabriel. "I have an idea who it probably was."

Lillian kept her eyes on the cup. She realized that Gabriel knew it was her.

"I know rules have to be obeyed," said Gabriel, "but the main thing is that we all take care of each other, right?"

Izzy smiled at him. "That's right."

Lillian looped her arm around Gabriel's waist. "I hope you never change, Gabriel."

"Don't worry about that, Mom. I won't. I'm just me. Can't change that."

"That's for sure," laughed Tommy.

"Tell them *your* news, Tommy!" cried Mickey with pride.

Lillian looked up. "You got your paper back?"

Tommy nodded. "I got an A."

"An *A*!" cried Mickey, as if that was nothing. "He got best paper for the whole 10th grade!"

Lillian jumped up and gave him a hug. "Tommy! I'm so proud of you." She looked at his beaming face and squeezed him again. "Wait till Charles hears!"

"Hail, Tommy!" cried Gabriel. "I'm going to start calling you Caesar. Or maybe Romulus. Romie!"

"Well done," said Izzy. "All you boys. Look at you." Her approving gaze fell on them all. "Doing well in school, working at jobs, volunteering. Good all-around boys. You would make any mother proud."

"But not *me*," Billy said, correcting her.

Izzy's head snapped back in surprise. "Of course, you!"

Billy gave a laugh. "Now I know you're joshing us."

Izzy took Billy's arm and gave it a light shake. "You listen to me. I've known you for a couple of years now, Billy Kinney. And I think you're a most remarkable boy."

A glimmer of hope filled his eyes, but he turned his head slightly, as if waiting for the catch.

"As a matter of fact," Izzy said, pulling him closer, "I have a sneaking suspicion that if I ever had a boy, he would be very much like you. A little on the wild side." She gave him a knowing wink.

"But – not a bad kid," Billy clarified, with some degree of doubt.

"Not bad at all. A very good kid. Smart, talented, with a great big heart!" Then, as if getting to the core of the matter, she added, "And a whole lot of fun."

Billy's face burst into happiness. "Did you hear that, Mickey?"

Mickey laughed and gave him a playful swat. "Course I did. Come on, guys. Dad's waiting for us."

Lillian and Izzy followed the boys to the door.

"Mickey, you have to tell Mom and Dad what Miss Izzy said." Billy turned around to explain. "They won't believe me if I say it."

"Come on," said Gabriel, dashing out the door. "First to the lobby is the winner!"

Izzy and Lillian watched with a smile as the boys raced down the stairs taking two at a time.

"Slow down! Don't make so much noise!" Mickey and Tommy urged, trying to overtake Billy and Gabriel.

Then – whether in preparation for the caroling, or as a result of Izzy's words of encouragement – Billy burst into the boisterous chorus from "Jingle Bells," joined by Gabriel. Then Mickey. Then Tommy.

Izzy laughed at their happy antics and smiled tenderly. "I hope mine turn out like that."

*

Lillian and Charles sat alone at the kitchen table, enjoying a rare dinner alone. Lillian got up to check on Charlotte, who was sound asleep on the living room rug with her blanket and toys.

"She wandered around looking for the boys," Lillian said. "Then gave up and fell asleep. She misses them when they're not here."

Over dinner, they continued their discussion about Izzy's news, and how she was worried about Red.

"He'll come through," said Charles. "A baby might be the best thing in the world for him. It will occupy his mind, force him away from – all that," he said with a general wave towards the past.

Lillian buttered a slice of bread and then stopped to look at it. "I read earlier about the long bread lines and the 'grim prospect' for Christmas in Vienna and all those places. The extreme food shortages, the threadbare clothes. It made me wonder if Mrs. Wilson isn't right. To adopt. To help one child. To do something. If everyone did…"

Charles took a deep breath and after a while said, "It's a much larger problem, global. And isn't going away anytime soon. The civil war resumed in China, guerilla battles in Indochina. The Arab-Israeli conflict. Rioting in India – they say partition is likely. The Greek civil war." Charles stared out and shook his head. "And the children get caught up in it all."

"One war always seems to breed the next, doesn't it," said Lillian.

"I think the old world order is changing. As it always does, with time. There's a shift, away from colonialism. A move towards independence, I think – I hope. The time of invading another country and taking it belongs to an earlier era."

Lillian stood and began to bring the dishes to the counter. After clearing up, Charles poured them both a small glass of port. They sat on the living room couch, watching Charlotte sleep amid her toys.

Lillian tucked her legs beneath her, a faraway look in her eyes. She took a slow sip of port. "Why do you think it keeps happening? War."

"I don't know," Charles replied, also taking a sip. "I'm afraid it's who we are."

Lillian couldn't accept that answer. It was too grim, too hopeless. "But we are also the lovers and the makers of beauty – the heroes and heroines of the everyday, aren't we? We love our children and want the best for them. We want the world to be a better place."

As if in support, an aria from Mrs. Taggert's Victrola drifted down the hall – a female voice reaching towards some ideal. Lillian had been vaguely aware of music in the background, but when the voice began singing "Casta Diva," she gave a soft sigh, as if balm had just been applied to her soul.

After taking a moment to listen to the stirring aria, Charles took Lillian's hand. "We are those things as well."

A soft smile came to his lips as he felt the longing and peace and beauty expressed by the voice. His eyes landed on the Roman history book, and the smile faded. "Our ideals and values must be protected. When they're not, greed and the demand for ever more power take over. And the empire crumbles."

"Rome?" Lillian asked, following his gaze.

"Rome. And all empires," he said wearily.

When the aria finished, Lillian took another sip and narrowed her eyes in thought. "Sometimes, I'm afraid that –" She left her thought unfinished.

"Afraid that what?"

She winced, not wanting to say it. "I'm afraid that some part of us likes it. War."

"There may be some truth to that," said Charles. "Especially in the beginning, when the idea of heroism, of being the defender, is intoxicating. Of everyone uniting and doing the right thing together. The problem is that both sides, or all sides, feel the same thing. And soon, they justify the violence, the killing." His face took on the haunted look that came when he remembered the war years, and for a while he was someplace else.

He made a low sound of contempt. "Why we create a living hell, over and over, is a mystery to me. There are enough survivors to remember the horror. The nightmarish horror. You'd think we'd at least wait longer, a hundred years or so, when the survivors are gone, and the warmongers can sell it afresh to a new generation." He shook his head and finished his port.

Lillian stroked his cheek and spoke in a lighter tone. "But for now, that's all over. And we can enjoy our children, our comfortable home." She filled her eyes with the Christmas decorations, Charlotte asleep with a doll tucked in her arms, and over at her alcove studio. "And my work. My art has helped me again and again. It anchors me."

"My work, too," said Charles thoughtfully. "I never realized just how important work is. It was always just something I had to do, like everyone else. But the truth is, my job helped me. Kept me focused. Pushed me to go farther, to challenge myself."

"I think that's why so many women – and some of the older men as well – have mixed feelings about losing their jobs now. I can't help thinking about Mrs. Wilson. That vague searching for something that is gone."

Lillian cocked her head, listening to the sound of footsteps running up the steps. "They're back," she said, and an air of happiness once again filled the apartment.

As the boys shook off their coats, they began recounting the highlights of the caroling, when Gabriel suddenly laughed. "Charlotte!"

They all looked over at Charlotte who was now sitting wide awake, quietly watching her brothers.

Tommy and Gabriel plopped down next to her, and Gabriel, always hungry, looked towards the kitchen.

"Is there any dessert left?"

While Lillian prepared a small plate of coffee cake and cookies, Charles waved the boys over to him, and whispered something. They nodded enthusiastically.

"I'm going to plug the Christmas tree lights in," Tommy said, when Lillian returned. "Charlotte likes it."

Lillian, still with a faraway look in her eye, smiled. "Good idea, Tommy. Let's have some Christmas cheer."

Charles took the plate of treats from her and set it on the coffee table. "The boys were just saying they'd like to give you an early Christmas present."

"An early present?" she asked, with a laugh. "Why?"

"Like you say, a bit of cheer is in order," said Charles. He whispered to Lillian. "It was Gabriel's idea. Let's go along with it."

"Oh! Well, if you want to…" She sat on the couch and looked at Gabriel, wondering if anything was amiss. But there he was, smiling as if he couldn't be happier.

Gabriel lifted various presents from under the tree, considering each one. Then Tommy said, "Let's save these for Christmas. How about that other one, in the bedroom?"

Gabriel shrugged. "Okay."

He came back with a very thin package and handed it to Lillian. "We were afraid Charlotte might break it so we hid it in our closet."

"You're being very mysterious." Lillian looked over to Charles, but he and Tommy were busy helping Charlotte with her blocks. Even Gabriel seemed half-hearted about the present. "You want me to open it?"

"Sure," said Gabriel, helping himself to another cookie.

Lillian opened the package and was surprised to see two records. She darted a glance to Charles and read the first cover. "Bing Crosby's 'White Christmas' and 'I'll be Home for Christmas.' She opened the second and exclaimed. "Oh! Nat King Cole's 'Christmas Song!'"

Gabriel smiled. "You said you liked that song about chestnuts."

"Yes, I do." Lillian looked up, slightly bewildered. "Why thank you, Gabriel. Tommy."

"We can ask Mrs. Taggert if we can play them on her Victrola," suggested Gabriel.

"Yes, we could do that." Lillian turned the albums over, feigning great interest. She gave an amused glance to Charles.

Tommy got up to stretch. "Guess I'll wash up. You want to go first, Gabe?"

"Nah. You can go." He held out his hands for Charlotte to toddle to him.

Lillian stood and brought the plate to the kitchen, puzzled by the rather anti-climactic present, but really, nothing Gabriel did any more surprised her.

She gave a light chuckle and turned on the kettle as she tidied up the kitchen. When the water was boiling, she took out a cup and saucer from the cupboard. "Does anyone want tea?" she called out.

She poured the water over the tea and added a spoonful of sugar. Again, she asked if anyone wanted tea. "Charles?" She waited for his answer. Then she turned her head to listen, hearing music again, but this time, clearer, and much closer.

All of a sudden, the velvety sounds of "Chestnuts" filled the air.

With the spoon still in her hand, Lillian came into the living room, wide-eyed, her mouth open in surprise.

"We forgot to mention the second part of your early present," said Tommy.

"It's a phonograph, Mom!" cried Gabriel. "And it's electric – you don't have to wind it up."

Charles went to her and gave her an embrace. "Merry Christmas!"

"Charles," she said softly, and hugged him and the boys. She went to look at the beautiful phonograph and the spinning disc and clasped her hands together. "How marvelous! Now we can have music whenever we want!"

"Happy early Christmas, Mom," said Tommy. "Dad said you wanted one of these."

"I don't know why I didn't think of it earlier," said Charles with a laugh.

"Now it really feels – and sounds – like Christmas," said Gabriel.

"It most certainly does!" Lillian leaned back against Charles, relaxed into his encircling arms, and let the music wash over her.

Gabriel went around turning off the lamps, until just the lights from the Christmas tree lit the room. "Charlotte likes it this way. It's more magical."

Charlotte had pulled herself up to the side of the couch and was moving back and forth, causing them all to laugh.

"Look," cried Gabriel – "she's dancing!"

Chapter 14

At breakfast, Charles ate a piece of toast at the counter and took a few sips of coffee while he hurriedly rechecked his briefcase. "I should be back by late afternoon. Give Mason time to go home and get ready for bowling."

Tommy helped to feed Charlotte, laughing at her noisy determination to feed herself, and Gabriel sat mulling over some idea, taking an occasional bite of oatmeal and toast.

Lillian sat with a cup of coffee and her notebook in front of her. She had made two columns, listing the pros and cons of staying at her current workplace or going with Mrs. Huntington.

For the past few days, she had spoken to Charles about her dilemma, about not wanting any more changes yet unsure about staying put, about her career as an artist. She had expressed her anxiety and her uncertainty, debating both scenarios. For the most part, she now realized, they were one-sided conversations. Charles had merely listened and smiled.

Stumped about what to do, she set her pen down, and looked up. "What are you so deep in thought about, Gabriel? Aren't you going to pick up Billy?"

Gabriel took a bite of toast. "Yep. He's coming with me to the Red String today. Mr. G said he could use some help on Saturdays for the next few weeks. He means it, but I also think he's trying to help Billy. Some people just like being kind. They're good at it. That's what I was thinking about."

"Like Mrs. Kuntzman," said Tommy. "And Mrs. Wilson. She always took our side whenever we got into trouble."

"And Miss Izzy," said Gabriel. "I've been thinking about what she said to Billy, about being a good kid. I know she *meant* it, but she didn't have to *say* it. It really mattered to Billy. Made him feel better about himself, you know?"

Lillian sat back and smiled. "It's amazing what a few words of kindness can do."

"Like you said to the hot chocolate vendor in the park the other day, Gabe," said Tommy, wiping jam from Charlotte's forehead.

"What'd I say?"

"You told him he has the best hot chocolate in the park. It made him happy."

"But I meant it."

"But you didn't have to *say* it."

Gabriel pushed his thoughts a little further. "Seems like a waste of happiness if it just stays inside you."

"So, you *said* it. Isn't that your point about Miss Izzy and Mr. G? Just like they didn't have to say how much they liked your skit – especially to Billy's parents – but they did."

"You're right," said Lillian. "And I think it made a difference. Billy's parents are going to let him take acting classes. That was quite a performance!"

Gabriel smiled at the memory. "Miss Izzy said she never laughed so hard."

"You two brought the house down," said Charles. "I even saw Red wiping tears of laughter from his face." He slipped on his coat and hat, and took a final sip of coffee. "See you later, boys. We'll have dinner at the bowling alley."

"Will they have fried chicken?" asked Gabriel, jumping up and following Charles. "I hope so. You know, I think I might be good at bowling."

"Not if it's anything like your cartwheels," Tommy called from the table.

Charles leaned down to give Lillian a kiss and glanced at her list. "I don't know why you're making it so hard on yourself. You've already made up your mind, haven't you?" He kissed Charlotte on the top of her head, the only jam-free place, and was gone.

Lillian held up her notebook, defending her process to whoever was listening. "Well. I think it's important to deliberate. To look at all sides before making a decision."

"But Dad's right, isn't he?" asked Tommy. "You're going to work for Mrs. Huntington."

"Of course, she is," said Gabriel. "Mom likes to work with nice people."

Lillian looked from one son to the other. "It's like the phonograph all over again. You all know something and are just waiting for me to catch up." She shut her notebook with a laugh. "All right. A change of plans for today. I'll still bring Charlotte to Mrs. Kuntzman, but instead of grocery shopping, I'll be heading downtown."

"To see Mrs. Huntington?" asked Tommy.

"Yes. I was thinking it would be nice to bring something for their new office, like a wreath."

"Oh, so you *did* know," teased Gabriel.

Lillian tweaked his nose. "I suppose I did. I had thought it might be at a future date. But I don't want to wait." She stood and gave a firm nod. "I'll go down to the Village, stroll around, and get a feel for the neighborhood. Then I'll stop by and say hello."

"You can take your time, Mom," said Tommy. "You won't have to worry about dinner. We'll be at the bowling alley. And Charlotte will be with Mrs. Kuntzman."

Lillian took his face in her hands and kissed his forehead. And then did the same to Gabriel. "How did I get such wise children?"

Tommy looked mildly embarrassed, and in a brisk manner remarkably similar to Charles's, he grabbed his coat, said goodbye, and left for his job at Mancetti's. Gabriel followed suit, and was soon on his merry way to the Red String Curio Store.

Lillian cleaned up Charlotte and dropped her off to the open arms of Mrs. Kuntzman who said she could watch her all day and evening, if Lillian liked. "And, I'll make a special dessert for youse all while she takes her nap. Custard." Lillian decided she would find a special present down in the Village for Mrs. Kuntzman. Dried berries or soaked cherries or candied fruit....

At the corner, Lillian noticed Mrs. Wilson up ahead. Her heart clenched as she watched the older woman walk one way, pause, look down in thought, and then walk briskly in the other direction. Still searching, still wanting.

Lillian watched her turn the corner, and understood that yearning for a life of meaning. She was grateful that she had found such meaning, had followed a many-detoured path, and that it had developed into a job, a career, a purpose. Work is good for one, Lillian thought, work is connection – to one's self, to others, to a larger cause. She hoped that one day Mrs. Wilson would discover the same for herself.

Lillian lifted her chin and took in a deep breath, sure that she was making the right decision. In one sense, she was stepping off into the unknown, unsure of what lay ahead. But she would be taking the journey with a trusted friend, and that made all the difference. The excitement that lay curled up inside her, just waiting to burst into being, was further confirmation that she was making the right move.

She would go into Haden Publishing next week and tell Mr. Borland of her decision. For now, she would indulge in the freedom of her new choice. A new beginning.

Down in the Village, Lillian took a few minutes to wander around, enjoying the cobblestone streets, the smaller buildings, the quaintness of the place. "I think I will love it here," she said, looking up at the decorated windows and fire escapes. From somewhere – perhaps a cracked open window – strains of a saxophone drifted over the street, and a smile came to her lips.

There was a different feel here, more artistic, charming. The people seemed different, too. Several women wore loose trousers, and had a Bohemian flair about them with scarves and shawls. She noticed berets and caps set at an angle, and many people with no hats at all. There was an easy individualism, tinged by a European influence. She knew that many refugees and political exiles lived in the Village, along with struggling artists and writers.

It was a more intimate, smaller world. She enjoyed walking past the second-hand bookstores, the coffee shops and jazz clubs, the interesting store fronts. Here was a vintage clothing store, with shiny ornaments and beaded garlands woven around the Victorian blouses and lacy white nightgowns. Next to it stood a tiny toy shop, with puppets and wind-up toys and a row of jack-in-the boxes, their jesters smiling in unabashed joy.

Lillian was drawn forward by an array of enticing scents – the sweet and smoky smell of roasting chestnuts, the comforting aroma of buttery pastries coming from the corner bakery, the scent of pine from the Christmas trees lined up for sale along the sidewalk and – she glanced up at the sky. Yes! that was it. Snow was on the way! It was going to be a perfect Christmas.

Lillian was suddenly eager to see Mrs. Huntington and the space that would be her new workplace. She couldn't wait to get started. She even hoped she could start next week! Smiling at her almost childish enthusiasm, she stopped at a small shop and bought a colorful tin of Christmas chocolates and a pine wreath tied with red ribbon. She was overflowing with Christmas cheer.

She soon found the address, and rang the bell. Lillian heard footsteps running down the stairs from the second-floor office. A harried looking Mrs. Huntington opened the door, and burst into a smile. "Lillian!" she cried.

"Do you still need an illustrator?"

"Do I ever!" She gave her a warm embrace and took the wreath, inhaling the pine scent. "Come in, come in!"

She introduced Lillian to the husband-and-wife team and another woman. Lillian immediately liked them all. Though they were extremely busy, running from one room to another, from desk to desk, putting together some layout, they took time to welcome her, offer coffee, and share the chocolates.

"Any chance you can join us for dinner?" Mrs. Huntington asked. "You'll love the French café on the corner. We could bring you up to date on our projects and talk about your role here. Oh, I'm so excited!" She gave her an impulsive hug.

"I'd like nothing more! And I'm completely free. Charlotte's with the babysitter and Charles is taking Tommy and Gabriel bowling tonight."

"Lillian, you've made my day! I couldn't be happier, and I can't wait to tell you all about our plans." She gave a nervous glance at the clock. "But right now what I need is another set of hands. We have a 6:00 deadline."

Lillian slipped off her coat, draped it over a chair, and rolled up her sleeves. "Put me to work!"

www.ingramcontent.com/pod-product-compliance
Lightning Source LLC
Chambersburg PA
CBHW030141010826
48973CB00002B/677